sportsball is for lovers

Neurospicy Book Club
Book Two

allie lasky

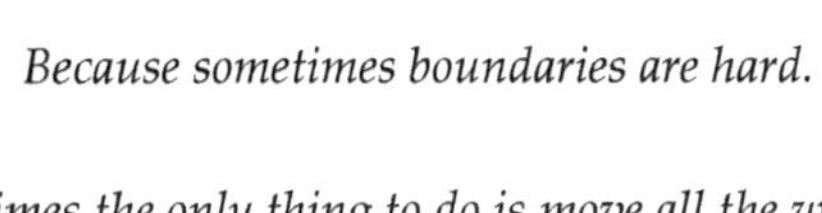

Because sometimes boundaries are hard.

Also, sometimes the only thing to do is move all the way across the country.

one

. . .

Sadie

august: tulsa

THE STRANGER'S hand fists in my hair, pulling my head back as his fat cock thrusts into me from behind, and my entire brain goes quiet.

"You like that?" he murmurs, his voice hoarse.

Letting out a whimper, I clench around his cock.

"I can't hear you." He tightens his grip in my hair.

"Yes." The word comes out breathy and light. "Please, sir."

The man fucking me groans. His other hand, on my hip, squeezes my flesh so hard I'm sure there will be a delicious bruise there in the morning.

I only have tonight. After sitting in meetings all day, it's nice to unwind a bit. Tomorrow, the conference will take up most of my day. After a quick dinner with friends, I board my flight home, and then it's back to my real life.

When I connected with J on the kink-based app, I didn't expect much to come of it aside from a quick hookup—wham, bam, and thank you, sir.

Instead, I found a man who fucks like a dream.

He's only in town for a moment, too. His profile says he's based in Denver, but he mentioned in our quick small talk that he's on the road a lot.

In real life, he's a thick, gorgeous man with caramel-colored skin about two shades darker than my olive tone, with a broad chest and soft belly covered in a healthy layer of well-trimmed hair. A Continuous Glucose Monitor is implanted on the back of his arm.

Our arrangement was quick: a seven-message exchange of location and details. Because we matched on the app after I scoped out his profile, I knew we'd theoretically be compatible in bed.

And as his hand moves from my hip to my ass, grabbing a generous handful and then giving me a solid smack, it turns out the app's algorithm got some things right.

I like what I like, and I'm not ashamed of it, nor should I be.

That doesn't mean finding a Dom who is actually good at taking care of my needs is an easy thing. Too many guys say they're a Dom but don't actually care about making sure their partner has a good time. They ruin it for the rest of us.

J, though—he's good at this. His hand lands on my ass again, slapping the jiggly flesh as his cock slides into me again and again. His belly rests against my ass, and the normal, human contact is reassuring. I don't need some chiseled bodybuilder wannabe Dom jerk. I need an actual guy who happens to have dominant tendencies.

The downside? It's one night only. I won't get this experience again.

He changes the angle, and as his cock hits my G-Spot, I let out a moan. Pleasure coils in my bloodstream and my hand moves to my clit to get me the rest of the way there.

"Did I say you could come?" he growls, pinning my hand to the bed.

That's what I gave him: my unconditional surrender. That's what he's expecting. That's what I have to offer.

Pulling out, he manhandles me onto my back, then holds my legs open and slides into me again with a shallow thrust. He gathers both wrists into his one-handed grasp, holding them above my head.

This is vulnerable. He has a full-body view now, all my rolls and cellulite and stretch marks. As much as I try to be confident, sometimes it's more difficult.

But as his dark eyes drink in the sight of my naked body, maybe I'm not giving myself enough credit.

Yeah, I'm big—but so is he. I'm not a delicate waif, but clearly that's not a problem for him.

With my hands pinned, the position pushes out my chest, and he leans down to my breast. His hand cups the large swell, massaging, and he sucks the tight bud of my nipple into his mouth. The light suction combined with the rasp of his tongue sends me climbing higher.

Finally, he touches me. His fingers on my clit are a welcome relief, and I moan so loud I'm sure the people three hotel rooms down can hear.

His touch is light, not nearly enough pressure, and I'm dead certain he knows that, the bastard. He smirks at me, his mouth on my breast, as I struggle against his grip.

He's got me.

His hips piston into mine, and as he finally relents and rubs me with firm, even circles, I finally, *finally* break. My skin feels extraordinarily tight. Pleasure courses through me and lights me up from my head to my toes.

All of a sudden, he pulls out, and I'm left clenching around nothing.

Throwing my head back against the pillows, I close my eyes tight, trying to keep the moisture at the corners from leaking. I am so goddamn frustrated I might spontaneously combust.

But then J is moving down the bed. He slides three fingers into me and lowers his mouth to my clit. The contact sends me spiraling again, or maybe still. As he puts pressure on my front wall and sucks on my clit, my hips move of their own volition, a desperate plea for *more*.

He releases my hands and immediately I move them to his hair, riding his face. The fist previously around my wrists moves to my face. His thumb traces my bottom lip and immediately I open, sucking the first two fingers into my mouth like I sucked his cock when this all began.

And then it's gone, and he's shifting, and suddenly his blunt, wet finger is pressing against my ass. I arch my hips up, and his dark eyes flit to mine, asking for permission. Checking for consent.

My profile says I'm down for anal, and honestly, right now, the way he's lighting up all my pleasure spots... I'm wound so tight, there is very little I'm not open to exploring with him.

"Do it." My voice comes out hoarse, broken.

Slowly, slowly, so fucking *slowly*, he pushes his fingertip inside. Not all the way—I'm not stretched, and saliva isn't adequate lube, but...

Pleasure erupts in my body like a firework, and I'm helpless to the sensations wracking my body. He keeps going even after I'm done, and as his finger presses further into my ass, the tremors go on and on forever.

Finally, I collapse, spent. I can't take any more.

J rises up onto his knees. His cock is still hard, an angry purple, and as he peels off the condom and wraps his fist around himself, I find myself suddenly interested again.

With a few quick strokes, he's spraying all over my chest. His release is hot and sticky on my skin, and he moves his mouth back to my clit, his tongue laving over my sensitive flesh hard and fast.

The second orgasm might be a continuation of the first. I

just know that I'm unable to do anything but ride the waves of pleasure coursing through me.

He drops onto the bed beside me, his chest heaving and his face red, a happy smile on his face.

Basking in the afterglow, I stretch from my head to my toes, pliant and loose. There's nothing like a good fuck to put me in a good mood.

After a moment, he rolls out of bed and disappears into the bathroom. He comes back with a wet towel. Kneeling over me, he thoroughly cleans me, then tenderly wipes his release from my skin.

His phone trills on the dresser, and he looks back at it with surprise.

"Wife?" I manage. My heart hammers in my chest.

He shakes his head.

"Girlfriend?"

"Work," he sighs. He presses his forehead to my thick belly, then exhales and forces himself upright. Scooping his pants off the floor, he gets dressed, tucking his dress shirt into his pants and throwing his suit jacket over his arm. "This was…"

"It is what it is," I tell him, heading off any platitudes. "I knew what I was getting into."

We met on a freaking kink app. We're both in town for a short period of time.

Of course it wasn't ever going to be anything more than easy, meaningless sex.

"I'll call you," he says.

Rolling my eyes, I pull the sheets up over me and snuggle into them. "No, you won't, and that's okay."

"If we're ever in the same city again…" He trails off.

"Yeah. Maybe."

The man I know only as J gives me a small smile, almost shy. "See you around."

two

· · ·

Sadie

six months later: boston

MY EYES HURT, my mouth is dry, and my head is pounding. I'm hungover.

But I haven't been drinking: I've been staring at my computer screen, pouring out the words all night long.

And now, after six weeks and ninety thousand words, I've got it: my book is finished.

Whew.

This one was rough.

"Shit, girl," Yoni says when he sees me. "You need a break."

"I'm fine," I tell my assistant—and, more importantly, my friend. "I can sleep when I'm dead."

With a snort, he opens the curtains, and I'm immediately assaulted by the bright winter sunlight reflecting off the snow-topped cars at street level.

"If you're not careful, that'll be sooner than you like," he warns.

Blinking my sore, red eyes a few times, I try to throw him a glare. "Why do you care?"

This time, Yoni laughs outright. "You sign my paychecks."

"Oh. Yeah."

Stretching, I reach upward, and my back cracks in several satisfying clicks.

"When's the last time you went outside?" he asks.

"Um… Sunday?" I had a shift at the bookstore, then took a few days off work to finish the book.

He rolls his eyes. "Great. Lovely. So you're getting up, taking a shower, and we're going for a walk."

"But—"

"You'll send the draft to Lu and then it will be out of your hands," he says firmly. "No sense in obsessing endlessly over something you can't physically do at the moment."

I make an unhappy face at him. "I don't obsess."

"*Bullshit*," he coughs.

"You're a poopy-face."

Yoni shrugs. "If that's what you tell yourself."

Turning to my computer, I save the file again, back it up, and email it to my critique partner without a comment. She's been expecting the book for a few days already. I promised it to her last week, which means I'm basically on time. Five days late is still on time, right?

"Okay." I yawn. "I'm going to take a shower, then we can go out."

"I'll start working on today's tackle list," he says, finally sitting down at his desk on the other side of the room.

Every day, Yoni makes a tackle list. He thinks a to-do list is so passé. It's things that absolutely have to happen today, the administration that goes along with being a semi-full-time author.

Okay. Not semi. Even though I work more than forty hours a week as a writer, I still have a full-time day job, too. As the manager of a local independent bookstore, I have a lot of flexibility, but I do still have responsibilities. I can't do it alone.

Enter Yoni. His best friend Asher is engaged to my best friend Arielle, and I genuinely like him as a friend, so when he was looking for a part-time gig six months ago, I brought him on. He helps me manage the admin stuff, packages and ships the books I've signed, and generally takes care of me.

I'm like his houseplant.

Except, you know, I'm a person.

Sometimes.

An hour later, freshly showered and hair washed, I feel a little more like myself. Taking my meds feels like coming up for fresh air. Even though I have a timer set to take them twice a day, sometimes I get distracted and forget what I'm doing when the alarm goes off. And then I *really* feel the effects of not taking them, which starts an endless cycle of self-hatred and doubt.

Yoni has cleared off my desk and made me a turkey sandwich. He's also filled my water cup. Seriously, I'm basically a houseplant.

"You're good at this," I tell him.

"Good at what?"

"Taking care of me."

He scrunches his face. "Don't be gross."

"Have you and Elliott thought more about—"

"No," he cuts me off.

"I'm serious, I'll do it," I offer again. I know I don't want kids, but I am fairly certain I'm willing to donate my eggs—to science, to someone who needs them. I just don't think I could also be his surrogate.

Luckily, he hasn't asked. I'm the one who offered.

"I'm just not ready to talk about it," he says. "When I'm in a better place."

His spouse, Elliott, wants a kid. Yoni is not so sure. I'm not sure if his reticence is because of the timing or the idea of caring for an actual child, but he's allowed some time to figure it out.

We all are.

And the more I think about it, the more I write stories about people falling in love and getting their happily ever afters… I'm not so sure if it's what *I* want anymore.

I mean—I want a partner. I want to fall in love.

But I don't know if I want all the things that go with it. The house in the suburbs with the kids and the minivan and…

I like living in the city. I like my job(s). I like my independence.

As it stands now, I'm traveling often. Between book signing events, writing retreats with my friends, conferences and seminars, I'm gone at least a few days each month, and then that's not including any personal travel to my family back home in Scottsdale.

Basically, I want a semi-long-distance relationship where the other person is okay with me virtually avoiding and/or ignoring them for days at a time. Where can I find that?

Even houseplants require some care and attention when I'm in the hyperfocus zone. That's why I have Yoni. What, am I going to get my assistant to communicate with my spouse for me when I can't look up from my manuscript? Is he going to coordinate dinner with my in-laws or send my nieces and nephews their Chanukah presents?

That reminds me—

"I have to go to Scottsdale." Yoni pulls out his journal to take notes.

"What's the occasion?"

"My parents' fortieth anniversary. My sisters are throwing a party."

He makes a face. "Does that mean I have to talk to them?"

"Talia and Sarah aren't that bad," I say carefully.

"What about Tamar?"

I laugh at the sneer on his face. He is *not* a fan of my third sister, and to be honest, I don't blame him. They've only met once, but the experience was unpleasant for everyone involved. She misgendered his spouse, who is nonbinary and uses they/them pronouns, and even after being corrected, Tamar continued to do it over and over again.

Talia, the oldest, and Sarah, the second eldest, are fine and pleasant. They're just in a different part of life than I am. I'm the youngest; the only one not married, the only one who doesn't have kids, the only one who has to work two and a half jobs to support herself.

The only one who doesn't live in Scottsdale.

I get itchy just thinking about returning to my hometown. Actually *being* in town? I'm lucky I don't have a panic attack every time I turn onto my parents' street.

There is nothing wrong with my family. They're *fine*. They're normal.

They're just… they don't really understand me. They've never really understood who I am and what I like. We don't have a lot in common.

There are multiple reasons I live across the country from them. Boston is my home now, not Scottsdale.

"It's not until June, but I know if I don't block out the time now, I'll forget to book the tickets until they're too expensive," I tell Yoni.

"And you'll need a hotel? Rental car?"

"Yes to hotel, no to car," I decide. I can't possibly stay at my parents' house. And with one of my sisters? No way. I can ride-share around town as I need to, that's easy enough, but I refuse to impose on them.

Because that's what it would be: an imposition. No matter what they say, I know the truth. They don't want me there.

He scribbles notes to himself, and I know that my part here is done; he'll take care of the rest, even setting up the reminders on my calendar, so all I have to do is show up.

Okay, and pack. I don't let him pack my suitcases. He puts away my grocery delivery, he's brought me supreme-ultra size tampons, but I can't stand the idea of him seeing my XXL granny panties.

We go for a walk and yes, it does feel nice to get some fresh air. Not that I'm ever going to tell the bastard that. When we get back to my apartment above the shawarma shop, he lingers in the doorway.

"You sure you don't want to come out with me?" Yoni asks. "I'm meeting my brother for dinner."

"I'm good, thanks. I don't want to impose." Mentally, I've moved on from my book-induced hyper-fixation, ready to curl up on the couch and scroll through Netflix for an hour until I give up and watch *The Princess Bride* again.

Yoni sighs. "You need to get out of the house."

"I went for a walk with you." I cross my arms over my chest.

"That's a start. Now keep doing it." He rolls his eyes. "It's not snowing, there's no frost warning, the wind chill is minimal. Get out of the house. Just for a little while."

"I could call Sullivan…"

"Yes, do that," Yoni says quickly. "You need to go out."

Sullivan is usually down to get a drink or three. Sometimes his girlfriend tags along—she's part of my Neurospicy Book Club, I love Johanna—but usually he and I will hit up a bar, he'll sketch and I'll write or doodle, and we'll pass the time peacefully. When Johanna joins us, she tends to read, leaving me and Sully to chill.

Arielle has Asher.

Rachel has Erik.

Yoni has Elliott.

Everyone is paired up, coupled up, and I have…

I don't even have a damn cat.

three

. . .

Jared

"SO TELL ME THIS AGAIN." I squint at my brother, like that will make his words any more clear. "You're doing what?"

We haven't seen each other in person in forever. My job has me on the road more than I'm home, and even when I'm in my apartment, I'm still halfway across the country from him. Even now, technically I'm in town on business—the team has an off day today, then tomorrow a game at seven o'clock, and it's right back onto the plane to hit the next city. Buffalo, I think. I don't really know. I just go where they tell me.

Yoni sighs. "I'm working for a writer."

"Yeah, not that part."

"We're going to a romance book convention in Denver next month," he says.

"Okay…"

"And it's the same weekend you have a home game."

I blink. "So?"

"So you should come to the convention. It's fun, I swear," my little brother says. "I only need to be there for set-up and tear-down, and the time in the middle I'm free for a few hours. There's hot, shirtless models." He waggles his eyebrows.

"Why do I think these models are more your type than mine?" I huff out a breath. "Do we have to actually *go* to the convention?"

"We can hang in the bar or something. The one I was at last month was like going to a youth group convention again, packed with awkward, drunk people in their sexual primes looking to get busy."

Pushing up my glasses onto my forehead, I pinch the bridge of my nose. "And you think this is fun?"

My younger brother has always been charming and outgoing. He's agreeable. He gets along with everyone. Whereas I… do *not*.

"It seriously is, dude," Yoni says. "Just give it a try. We'll be in Denver next month, then a month later we're in Nantucket, a few weeks later another in Charleston, and there's one more event in Minneapolis before she goes away to her writing retreat."

"And you *like* this? Being an assistant?"

He shrugs. "I enjoy what I do."

"You can still—"

"I'm not going back to school, Jared," he says, his voice steely.

Holding my hands up innocently, I shake my head. "I wasn't going to suggest—"

He gives me a hard look. "You want me to go back to school. You know being a dentist was Mom's dream for me. It was never mine."

"You can use your biochem degree for other things, though. It doesn't have to be dentistry," I point out.

"I'm fine. I'm paying my bills. Supporting myself. El and I—"

"How are they?" To avoid a fight, I purposefully shift the conversation. "Are they coming on the trip out there?"

Elliott couldn't make it tonight; they had a late meeting at work they couldn't get out of. It's okay. I'll see them tomorrow for lunch before I have to get ready for the game.

My brother is great. His spouse is awesome. I couldn't be more happy that my little brother found the person that makes him feel like the best version of himself.

Even if I feel like the worst version of myself right now...

Yoni shakes his head. "Nah, they have work. And this is work for me and Sadie."

"I thought you said her name was Sylvie."

"Sylvie is her pen name."

"What, is she eighty years old?" I joke.

He gives me a hard stare. "It was her great-aunt's name, of blessed memory. She was the only person in her family who gave a shit about her."

Immediately, I feel remorse. "Sorry."

"Don't be a dick," Yoni chides. "You're better than that, Jare."

With a sigh, I run my hand over my ears, adjusting the thick black stems of my glasses frames. It's crazy how my little brother can make me feel so small.

Not that either of us are so little. Yoni is maybe an inch or two taller than me, and even though we're on opposite sides of thirty, we're both sporting a spare tire and then some around the waist.

When we were kids, our mom was always shopping in the *husky* section of the store, and no matter how much I diet and exercise, I can't seem to shift the weight. The diabetes diagnosis a few years back didn't help much—it means I have to be even more conscious of my intake, and considering how often I travel for work, where only junk food is available at arena concession stands...

Who am I kidding? I can make excuses all I want. The fact remains, I have Type II Diabetes, it's not curable but it is manageable, and my entire life is different now.

"So tell me about what you do. What do you like about it?" I ask.

Yoni eyes me curiously.

"I'm serious. I want to know. Something is obviously drawing you to it, and clearly you're good at it, so explain it. Help me see what you see."

He blows out a breath. "I'm not that creative," he says.

"Yonatan," I snap.

As I expected, he winces at the usage of his full name. When I was little, I used to call him Yo-yo. Now, I reserve Yonatan for when it really matters.

"No, I'm not," he interjects. "I'm smart, I'm good at math and science, but I'm not creative and I'm definitely not artistic. Sadie... She creates this world, this entire universe of characters that I want to be part of. She weaves the details so it looks effortless. But seeing the day to day, I see how much work goes into it, I see the effort it takes to make it look so easy."

He sighs. "And I like being part of something bigger than myself. She needs grounding, balancing, or else she floats away in the clouds."

"And you want to ground her?" I ask.

Yoni shrugs. "I mean... I like taking care of her."

My eyebrows go up.

"Not in a sexual way," he's quick to assure me. "I'm committed to Elliott, and even if I weren't, I would still never be attracted to a woman."

Chewing the inside of my cheek, I wonder how much I should reveal about my own sexuality to my brother. Even though I consider myself Dominant, I'm what people call a "soft Dom," where I get off on praising my partner and taking care of them instead of degrading them.

I want to make my partner feel good, and that extends beyond the bedroom. My whole world narrows down to my partner, to taking care of them and making sure they're okay.

I don't necessarily need to be called *Daddy*—though it definitely doesn't bother me.

I'm not in this to get my rocks off and move on to the next. There's a deep-rooted need in me that gets satisfied by bringing my partner to the brink of pleasure again and again. The brain chemical cocktail called Domspace is a high like none other, and actually *finishing* has the unfortunate tendency to end the brain chemicals.

Since I'm on the road so much, I don't have the time or inclination for a permanent, long-term relationship. I stick to one-night-only flings with whoever I can match with on my favorite kink app. It's discreet, the algorithm is fairly robust, and it works for me.

I decide against saying anything to Yoni about all that. My brother and I, we don't talk about sex. Aside from the time I caught him making out with a guy in his bed when they were in high school, that is. I reminded him that just because they couldn't get each other pregnant didn't mean it was safe to skip the condoms and bought him a beginner's toy—and a giant bottle of lube, so he wouldn't steal mine. I didn't out him to our parents, though. When he was ready, he told them.

Once, he walked in on me and my ex-fiancée in a... compromising situation in our kitchen. We didn't talk about that. He went red, turned away, and then refused to look me in the eye for the rest of the long weekend.

Okay—calling it compromising is a bit of a stretch. She was wearing a dress and her panties were around her knees, my pants were barely undone, and I was buried balls-deep inside of her, pinning her to the kitchen island. But he couldn't *see* anything with the kitchen island between us.

Fuck. I don't miss Candace, I really don't, but she was fun to play with. She's the one who got me into the *scene*. Ultimately, our lifestyles weren't compatible, even if our kinks were on paper.

She wanted to have our kids baptized and raised in the

church, and that was something I just couldn't cave on. Even though I'm not sure I want children, if I were to have them, I would absolutely want them to be raised in the same secular Jewish culture I was.

For now, though… it's all hypothetical.

"I'm happy, Jare," Yoni tells me as the waiter delivers our shared dessert. "I really am."

"That's all I want for you, Yo-yo."

He smiles and looks down at his drink, hesitation written on his face.

"What's up?" I ask.

"El wants kids," he blurts.

I sit back. "Oh."

"And I…"

"Do you?" I ask gently.

"I think?" My brother looks like he's guessing at a geography question and not a life-altering decision.

"You kind of need to be sure about this."

"I know." He sighs. "I'm not… I *want* kids, I do, but I don't think it's the right time, and there's the money involved in egg donation and then a surrogacy, and I just…" He blows out a breath.

"It's a lot." My words are quiet.

He nods. "It is. I'm not saying no, you know? I just—not right now."

"If not now, when?"

Yoni rolls his eyes at me. "Don't quote Rabbi Hillel at me."

I pause—and then repeating the words to myself, I laugh. It's a famous Jewish proverb. "I swear I didn't intend to."

He seems a little more relaxed, though. "We've only been married for a year and a half," he points out. "I think we need to be a little more established together."

They got married quick; from first date to engagement was seven months, and then the wedding was three months later. They were happy. They *are* happy.

But that doesn't mean they need to jump into the next step if either of them aren't ready.

"It's okay to do things in your own time, and they should be supporting you in figuring out a timeline that works for both of you."

"What about you?" Yoni asks me.

"What about me?"

"Do you have any plans?"

"Like...?" My eyebrows lift.

"Like when are you going to date someone for longer than a week?" he snarks.

I don't take his words as the cutting remark he intended. "When I'm not on the road for eight months a year," I fire back. "But until I can get an in-studio job, I kind of have to go where the work goes."

"You could do long distance," he points out. "Plenty of people—"

"I'm not interested," I tell him honestly. "I don't like having to keep up with and check in on anyone. I'm selfish. I want to prioritize myself and my career for now."

"There are apps..." He trails off.

"I'm on the apps. I go out and hook up plenty, don't worry." My smug smile makes him groan and roll his eyes.

He does give me an idea, though. Pulling out my phone, I turn on location services and the app starts finding people in the city whose profiles indicate they would be an ideal match.

A picture of an excellent pair of tits pops up on my screen. A small birthmark on her clavicle tickles my memory. I chew the inside of my cheek, thinking.

"What's up?" Yoni asks.

"I think I hooked up with this woman before," I say slowly.

"Was it good?"

"Well, I didn't block her after, so..."

He shakes his head. "Sometimes I forget you're a dick."

"I don't even remember what city it was." Scrolling through the chat history from October, I have a vague recollection.

"You going to see her?"

I shrug. "Might as well. Don't have anything better to do."

Tapping out a message, I send it, and the three dots at the bottom of the screen dance as she types her reply.

"So? What's she say?" Yoni raises his eyebrows.

Smirking up at him, I slip my phone back into my pocket. "Looks like I've got a date tonight after all."

four

. . .

Sadie

SULLIVAN IS WAITING in our favorite booth when I walk into the bar. Nodding to Jack, the bartender, I greet my friend with an enigmatic smile.

"What did you do?" he asks, pushing aside his sketchbook.

"I need you to do something for me."

He glowers at me. "Why should I?"

"You'll get something out of it," I insist.

Sullivan rolls his eyes. "So? What is it?"

"I need you to go home tonight and fuck your girlfriend."

He blinks at me. "I will, thanks, babe. Why the fuck—"

"I need you to butter her up, and I need you to ask her to design my next cover," I continue.

He snorts, shaking his head because he is *so* used to my bullshit.

"Yeah, okay. I'm not talking to her about you in bed, though."

"Whatever it takes. I *need* her help."

"You do realize she has a full-time job."

I shrug. "She's good at what she does. She could do it full-time if she wanted. I've got connections for her."

Johanna is a graphic designer, and she's fucking awesome at what she does, there's no doubt about that. She's done graphics for me and I've commissioned some artwork. There are plenty of full-time cover designers in the indie author space—and even more who do it as a side gig, so she could keep her day job if she wanted. She's already a huge romance reader, too; it would be a logical progression.

"She doesn't want the side hustle." Sullivan sips his drink. "I'll talk to her, though."

Jack delivers my beer, squeezing my elbow before he returns to the bar.

"So what's new with you?"

I've been in a self-imposed cocoon for the last few weeks while I finished the book. Aside from my shifts at the bookstore, I barely left my house, and the end result is a book I'm freaking proud of. It might be my best yet.

"Nothing crazy," my bestie says. "Work shit, family shit, life shit…"

It's my turn to roll my eyes. "Wow. Lovely. Informative."

He grins. "Yeah, I am lovely, thank you."

Lifting my beer to my lips, I take a sip, then sit back with a happy smile. Sullivan and I are an unlikely pair, I know. He's a good guy. And he's involved in the book world, so we have professional connections in common. I'm so glad I ran into him at that publishing convention last year and basically forced him to be my friend. He dotes on Johanna, who is part of my Neurospicy Book Club at the store. He's a good bud to have.

There's a spring training baseball game on the TV across from us. My face scrunches and I turn away. I deal with baseball enough in my work life, I don't want to spend my free time thinking about it, too. Even if my team is purely fictional.

Sometimes it pisses me off to no end that I wrote a series

of baseball romance novels, because now I can't enjoy watching a game the same way. It's work.

Although… I tilt my head as a new story idea flirts with my brain.

"You good?" Sullivan asks.

I squint at him. "What would you do if your best friend virtually dumped you when you got drafted to different teams, and now ten years into the league you're suddenly on the same team?"

"Well, I'd fuck him, clearly," he says.

Sullivan is the most heterosexual male I know. He's gone to gay clubs with his brother for years, playing wingman for Theo before he met his now husband. He's also fully devoted to his girlfriend, who he pined over for years.

But I write queer romance, and he knows that, so I appreciate that he's playing along.

"Actually…" He sips his beer. "That kind of happened with me and my buddy Miles. We were friendly growing up, went to different high schools, and then we played for the same college team. We didn't hang out even then. It wasn't until we graduated that we really became friends again."

"Were you upset with him when you reconnected?"

He shrugs. "I had my head up my ass. I was thoroughly in my slutty phase, he was in his insecure hermit phase, and we both had to grow up a bit beyond that to see eye to eye. We're good now, though. I stood up in his wedding last fall."

My brain whirrs with buzzing thoughts. It's a quirk of neurodivergence; sometimes it feels like my brain is a separate entity from myself. Even though my therapist is convinced I don't have a personality disorder, every few months I fall down a spiral of self-doubt. Juggling the "real me" Sadie with my work persona of Sylvie is hard enough.

That's the downfall of being a hypochondriac with absent-minded tendencies. I forget we've already ruled something out and convince myself I have whatever new diagnosis I see.

Sullivan says something, and I shake my head, not ready to hear him. I'm too distracted by the shiny new story idea percolating in the background of my mind.

After a few moments of chewing on the thoughts, I pull out my notebook and start scribbling down ideas. This is one of the hazards of being a writer; inspiration can strike at any time, even if I'm not ready for it. It's really fucking fun, though.

My phone buzzes on the table in front of me. Flipping it over, I read the display, and a fizzle of heat rushes through me.

"What's up?" Sullivan asks.

It's J. The guy from Tulsa. It's been ages since our seriously hot hookup.

What's the chance you're in Boston tonight? His message burns through me.

I live in Boston, I reply back. The app is telling me he's seven miles away.

Want to meet up?

"Oh, shit," Sullivan says, interrupting my thoughts. "Some dude?"

Nodding, I bite my lip, processing.

"You going to see him?"

I had a perfectly nice time with J in our one night together. I wouldn't be opposed to repeating…

Can't host. I can come to you, I text back. I never invite one-night stands back to my place.

In response, he sends me a pin to a hotel in Fenway-Kenmore. *Seeing my brother for dinner. Should be free by 9.*

I send him a thumbs up in reply and pick up my beer again, taking a sip to calm down my seriously warm face.

I haven't gotten laid in—was Tulsa the last time?? That is very much atypical for me. Work has been seriously full-on; I've barely had time for myself, much less my friends or a hookup.

Tonight? Oh yeah, I'm going to get mine.

"Get it, girl," Sullivan says, seeing my smirk. He lifts his beer against mine. "May he give you all the screaming Os you deserve."

"So like, twenty?" I grin.

He shudders.

"Okay, I'll settle for three. Maybe four," I concede. I already know J can deliver.

"We'll get together next week for a debrief," Sullivan promises.

five

· · ·

Sadie

A FEW HOURS LATER, I'm getting out of a ride-share at the hotel, wearing a knee-length coat, high-heeled leather boots, and a killer lingerie set beneath my simple leggings and sweater. As much as I'd like to show up in nothing but a bra and panties beneath my coat, it's also eleven degrees outside, so I dressed for the weather rather than sex.

The sex will come later.

When I told J I was on the way, he sent me a room number, so I bypass the front desk and head directly to the fourth floor and knock on room 1438.

The door swings open almost immediately, and I'm treated to the intoxicatingly handsome stranger I met all those months ago in Tulsa.

"Fancy meeting you here," J says, his warm, chocolate brown eyes drinking me in.

"How about that," I tease back.

He takes a step back, wordlessly inviting me into his hotel room, and I follow as if hypnotized.

Also, I really fucking want to.

He's even more gorgeous than I remember. His winter-pale skin is still a few shades darker than my own and his dark hair has grown out a bit compared to our previous meeting. He's wearing the same black plastic glasses frames and short beard. His jeans and button-down shirt are simple, casual, without being unkempt.

"So you're in town for a bit?" I ask, taking off my coat and tossing it onto the desk.

His eyes drink in my curves. "I leave tomorrow night."

"That's a shame." I whip my sweater over my head, revealing my black lace bra. "Guess we'll have to make the most of our time together, then."

He moves toward me, caging me in against the dresser. His scent, spicy and fresh, surrounds me, and I can't help but close my eyes as I try to savor the sensory overload.

"Sober?" he asks.

My eyes flutter open. "I had two beers over three hours," I report back.

He nods, rubbing the thick layer of stubble on his chin.

"I'm not reading into this," I tell him.

J raises his eyebrows.

"We matched on the app. It tells you when you're within a certain distance of another person with a matching kink. That's all this is."

He threads his hands through my hair, finger coiling around a particularly spirally wave.

"And if it's not?" he asks, his voice quiet but firm. My stomach flutters.

"You're only passing through. Let's not pretend it's more."

J cups my face, tilting my chin up. I rise onto my tiptoes and he kisses me. This is too sweet, too gentle for a spur-of-the-moment hotel room hookup.

Pulling back, I'm ready to give him a piece of my mind. I signed up to be fucked by a Pleasure Dom, not this lovey-dovey bullshit.

"What the fuck is this?" I demand.

J tilts his head, squinting at me. "Excuse me?"

"'This." I swirl a finger at his face. "I thought you were going to fuck me."

To my surprise, he laughs. "Don't worry, babe, I will. Give me a fucking chance."

My hands go to my hips. "A chance to what? Fall for me? I'm not interested in that—"

J's mouth crashes down on mine. He lets out a rumbly sound that vibrates through me and I sway against my will, my body wanting to meld with his.

My hands fist in his shirt, the starched material refusing to crumple. His pecs are wide and hard with a little give to them. He's not some ultra-obsessive gym rat who doesn't have any brain space for anything other than working out. He's… normal.

And as his tongue slips into my mouth, I feel the desire of his kiss from my head to my curling toes and everywhere else in between. He forces me to be in the moment instead of lost in my thoughts.

My thoughts are comfortable. I like being there, consumed and distracted all at the same time. In the present? I'm forced to *feel* things.

I don't like feeling things. In fact, I almost think I'm allergic to it.

J deftly unhooks my bra and flings it to the side. His hands cover my breasts, the swells flowing over his big palms. I'm not a spritely little thing, but he doesn't seem to mind.

He walks me back toward the bed. The back of my knees hit the mattress and without hesitation, I sink down onto it. This puts me in direct line of sight with his dick.

The crotch of his jeans is tented by the large bulge. My mouth waters and I move to undo his belt.

"Ah, ah," he teases, plucking my hands away. "Did I say you can touch?"

The head rush I get… My eyes close as I try to regain any

sense of equilibrium. This is what I want. This is what I asked for.

"Please, sir," I beg, and the words come out breathy. "Please may I touch you?"

J studies me, his head cocked.

Anticipation boils in my bloodstream, lighting me up from the inside.

"Take my cock out and suck it like a good girl," he orders.

My fingers shake as they work at his belt and then his zipper, drawing out his thick length.

My mouth waters as I wrap my fingers around him. The vein on the underside of his cock pulses when I press my thumb against it.

His sharp inhalation sends a burst of happiness to my core. I want to please him. I want to make him happy. Here, where it's just the two of us in our little sex bubble, I can be whoever and whatever I want.

And right now, I don't want to think. I don't want to decide. I just want to *be*.

His hips flex forward and I bring my mouth to the tip of his dick, lapping at the pre-cum accumulated in his slit. It's salty and rich. My eyes roll back in my head, the familiar tang lighting up my pleasure center.

He likes this.

And when I suck the head of his cock into my mouth, tongue swirling around the swollen tip, he lets out a soft sigh that tells me I'm doing good.

My hand strokes the parts of him I can't fit into my mouth. I slip a hand under to cup his balls, rolling them in my hand.

His hand falls to the back of my head, fisting the waves there. J doesn't exert pressure; he just lets me know he's there, he's got me, or maybe I've got him.

As I fall into a rhythm, so does he, his hips pushing forward into my mouth, and I relax my jaw to let him fuck my face.

J snaps his hips forward, his cock nudging the back of my throat, and he holds there until my eyes water and saliva drips down my face and I start to gag.

That's when he pulls out. He pushes me back onto the bed.

He's still wearing his jeans. Quickly removing them, he pulls a strip of condoms and a small bottle of lube from his pocket, tossing them onto the bed.

I pick up the strip of three latex squares. "Ambitious, much?"

J smirks at me, his eyes bright. "Hopeful."

I know he has killer stamina, but given that he's in his early thirties, I would have assumed his refractory period would be longer than that.

"We don't have to use them all tonight," J adds.

"I thought this was a one-night-only thing?"

He laughs. "That was last time. Now it's this time."

"So…"

"I want you to stay," he says softly.

I pause. That's not what I signed up for. There's no sleep-overs when it comes to anonymous app hookups. Bing, bang, boom, we're done.

Although… it's, like, eleven degrees out. I don't mind staying in the warm hotel room for a little while longer.

"I'll stay," I finally tell him.

His unguarded smile blooms warmth inside my chest.

Oops. That's not what this is supposed to be about. No feelings, just fucking.

I need to get this back on track before I derail. I'm here to be railed into next week. That's all I want from him. Nothing more.

I can't have anything more.

"But first," I announce, ripping off a square, "I need you to fuck me."

six

. . .

Jared

WHEN I WAKE UP, she's gone.

Fuck.

Then I hear the water running in the bathroom, and a few moments later, she's back in my line of sight, fully nude.

My sharp intake of breath startles her, and she blushes.

"I should go," she says.

Shaking my head, I reach for her hand and pull her back to the bed. She stays on her side of the bed, and I rest my head on the pillow, admiring the curves of her full breasts and the soft, downy skin of her belly.

"Only if you want to," I tell her. "I'm not rushing you out."

She raises her eyebrows. "Really?"

I nod. "I like this. I like you."

She sighs. "Yeah. If only you didn't live so freaking far away."

"I'm not cut out for anything permanent," I admit. "I'm always on the road…"

"No, I get it," she says. "It's nice and convenient when we're in the same city, but we both have our own lives."

Glancing at the clock on the nightstand, I do a quick calculation. "I have two hours before I have to leave for work. Want a goodbye fuck?"

Her cheeky grin is answer enough.

An hour and a half later, when we're curled up in bed and breathing hard, I start to let myself hope. I wonder what it would be like to have this all the time.

I think I want it. I don't know how to get it, much less *maintain* a relationship like this, but I really like the idea of it.

My brother is happy. My friends are happy.

Why can't I be happy, too?

"I wish I could stay," I murmur as my hand learns the curve of her arm.

She turns her head away. "Don't make this more than it is."

I tilt her face toward mine. "I mean it. I wish I could."

"Yeah, well, I live here, and you live wherever the fuck you do, so…"

She gets out of the bed and starts to pull on her clothes.

Fuck. I'm doing this wrong.

"What's with the cold shoulder?"

She shrugs. "If I convince myself I don't want to sleep with you again, it won't hurt so much when I never see you again."

I cross to her and tip her chin up. "We could, though…"

"How? Why?"

"I mean…"

S shakes her head. "I don't want a relationship. Neither do you. It was written clearly in our profiles. No strings attached. It was a bad idea to meet up again."

"Things change."

"Do they, though?" She tilts her head at me. "Or are you just high off the orgasm endorphins?"

I might be.

I seriously might be.

But something is telling me there's more to this, more to us, than just a two-night stand.

I want more.

Do I want more with her? Or will any random woman do?

No. It's S. There's something about her that's making alarm bells go off in my brain.

I'll probably never see her again. There's no reason for our paths to cross. She lives here, and even though I live in Denver, I'm on the road so much, I spend more nights in generic hotel rooms than in my own bed.

No, I don't think I can sustain a relationship right now, especially not long distance. I need to focus my energies inward. That's more important right now.

If I don't put myself first, nobody else will.

———

The intern has been stuck to my side like glue. I don't even know his name. I should probably know it by now, except he wears his name badge affixed to his waist rather than around his neck or on his lapel like the rest of us.

Gen, my boss at the studio, does not look pleased with this development.

"Can I talk to you?" she mutters, jerking her head toward the conference room.

That's never good.

Pushing away from my desk, I go to follow her, and like a lost puppy, the intern follows us.

"This is between me and Aviyente," Gen says, and I fucking *hate* the way she can't pronounce my last name. It's not that difficult. Ahv-ee-yen-tay.

It's not that much different from other Spanish names. My family was originally from Spain and Portugal, with a brief stop in Morocco before immigration to Israel, and then my dad moved to the US when he was a kid.

Because I'm brown but don't have a noticeable accent, I get a lot of pointed questions about where I'm from—and when I tell them Tacoma, they say, no, but where am I from *originally.*

People don't always understand that being Jewish is both a religion and an ethnicity. Ethnically, my family is Jewish. Culturally, I grew up Jewish. Religious beliefs... those are a little more difficult to parse out. I definitely believe in the stories I grew up learning, even if I don't actively practice the religion day in and day out.

The good thing about this country is that there is no national religion or ethnic background that is superior. Sure, some people may try to legislate it as if there were, but at least for now, there is no national edict that says my ethnic background and my belief system are wrong or illegal.

Gen sits across from me in the conference room, staring like she's said my name already.

Clearing my throat, I adjust my tie and settle in my seat. "What's going on?"

"You're too critical," she says.

My eyebrows go up. "Of?"

"The team. We know they're not playing well," she says flatly. "You don't have to rag on them every night."

I tilt my head. "I'm not ragging on them. I'm informing the public of their play."

"Yeah, well, spin it in a better light."

"Like... how?" I'm genuinely confused. "Do you want me to use more statistics or lean more on the play analysis? Focus on the team dynamic?"

Denver's hockey team isn't last in the league—they're third from the bottom, thank you very much.

"I don't know," Gen says, throwing her hands up in the air. "Just do better!"

"How do I know what to change? I don't know what the station wants."

"I told you. Stop being critical."

"But the team isn't winning," I remind her.

"No shit."

"So how do I talk about the team without mentioning the fact that they've lost seven of their last nine games?"

I don't know what she wants from me. I don't think *she* knows, either.

"Well, if you don't turn it around, Todd will be in your chair this time next week."

"Who's Todd?"

Gen glares at me. "The intern."

Oh.

Oh, *shit*.

seven

. . .

Sadie

WHEN I STEP into the hotel lobby, a sense of peace washes over me. I'm home.

Even though, you know, a grubby hotel in suburban Denver isn't exactly *home*.

There's a banner welcoming readers and writers to the 7th Annual Book-a-holics Convention. Kira, the daughter of one of the event organizers, is sitting behind a small table with a bunch of packets spread on the table in front of her.

"Sylvie!" Kira looks up and grins at me. She's about nineteen and an absolute delight. "I'm so glad you made it!"

"Oh, I wouldn't miss it for the world," I tell her sincerely. "How's your mom? Is she scrambling yet?"

Kira laughs. "You know her. If she's not frantic, it's only a matter of time."

Rosemary, one half of the event organization team, is a little prone to panic. How she makes a living as an event organizer, I've never been able to understand. The constant stress and anxiety would drive me nuts.

When Rose isn't planning events, she's making a decent career as an independent author. In her spare time, she designs covers and formats books for other authors, as well as knits and crochets small dragons and dinosaurs. She is supremely talented.

I've known her for about eight years. She was one of the first friends I made on the author circuit, and her events are a mainstay in my schedule every year. Her other half of the business, Andie, lives a few hours from me in New Hampshire, and we get together for weekly coffee dates online and monthly writing group sessions in person.

Kira hands over my packet and gives me a rough rundown of the itinerary. Most of these events run the same: Friday afternoon starts with a happy hour in the hotel bar, a meet and greet with readers, and usually most of the authors head back to the bar.

On Saturday morning, we get into the ballroom about two hours before the event starts to set everything up, and sometimes, it takes the full two hours just to get your wagon or dolly full of books into the elevator. Then there's an admittance for early readers, a break for lunch, and then the full signing event. In the evening, there's a party. It's almost like being at a bar mitzvah party for adults; there's a DJ, a well-stocked bar, and a bunch of socially awkward introverts sitting by themselves reading a book or playing on their phones.

After we check in and grab our room keys, Yoni and I head up to our shared hotel room. I could totally spring for a second room for him, but he doesn't mind sharing, and honestly, after paying his salary, his admission to the event, his airfare, and his meals, *all* on top of my travel expenses... I'm lucky to break even on the event. Hell, usually I lose money on these types of weekends.

But it's not about the money. It's the experience. I love getting to connect with readers, and having a chance to see my online friends in real life is always amazing. I've fostered so many great relationships in the last eight years since I impulsively published a book online.

Now, it's a career.

Not a financially viable one, but a career nonetheless.

Upstairs, we both unpack: I take out my outfits, steam them, and hang them in the closet, and he unloads the boxes of books and supplies into neatly organized piles. When we're done, we both crash onto our separate double beds.

"You good?" Yoni turns his head, looking over at me.

"I'm good," I tell him. "Take your nap. I'm going to go visit with Rose, see if she and Andie need any help."

He yawns. "Mmkay."

With a laugh, I force myself upright and freshen up before heading back downstairs. In the event center, Rose is directing a slew of volunteers, and Andie is methodically picking at the nonexistent split ends of her hair.

Suddenly, I'm tackled from behind, and arms wrap around my waist.

"Hey, boo," LuAnn says into my ear, then laughs.

Turning in the circle of her arms, I hug her back. "You're a real person!" I touch her face, and she grins back at me.

Lu is my critique partner, my best friend, and an all around awesome person. She's a mid-forties aromantic lesbian who writes some of the *dirtiest* male/male smut I've ever seen. Sure, she also writes sapphic fiction and heteronormative romance, but her money-maker is the guy-on-guy action.

Unfortunately—and this is the single worst thing about her—she has the audacity to live in North Dakota, which means I don't get to see her in person often enough for either of our liking.

We met in an online publishing forum about five years ago and struck up an instant friendship. We write in separate subgenres, she's fifteen years older than me, we're in entirely different stages of our lives and author careers… It doesn't matter; she's my bestie, my ride or die.

"How was your flight?" she asks, slinging her arm around me.

"Great. No delays. Yours?"

"A little bumpy." Lu shrugs. "My books made it, which is all that matters."

The last signing we went to, her luggage didn't arrive in the airport on time, so she scrambled at the last minute. It's not always feasible to ship books to the host hotel ahead of time. It was a *whole* thing.

Lu and I chat for a bit, and as more of our friends arrive, we greet them and catch up. It's a weekend-long party. These people are my friends. My coworkers. My community.

After a while, it's time to get ready for the evening. Yoni is in bed scrolling on his phone when I get back to the room.

"Have a good nap?" I ask him.

He nods, his eyes still sleepy. "Thanks for letting me."

I scoff. "I don't let you do anything. Aside from the hour I need you tomorrow, you're free to do whatever you want."

Yoni sits up. "In that case, is it cool if my brother comes to visit tonight?"

I know he wanted to see his brother tomorrow during the event.

"Sure. The more, the merrier. It's open admission." As I grab my bag, I turn back. "You okay if I take a shower first?"

He nods. "Go ahead."

Running through my routine, I wash my hair and style my curls for presentation.

Calling them curls is a bit generous. My hair is wavy, and with a lot of product and manipulation, I can get soft curls for a few hours. By tomorrow morning, they'll already be flat waves, so I'll redo it for the event. Normally, I don't wash my hair two days in a row, but when I have to be "on" and presentable…

Yoni takes his turn in the shower as I apply my makeup and finish getting ready. My outfit for tonight is a silky gray dress with a low-cut neck, floor-length hem, and gauzy sleeves, and it makes me feel like a floaty princess. I've paired it with olive green heeled booties—my favorite.

As I'm trying to fasten my necklace, there's a knock on the door, and expecting Lu, I open it to find the most handsome guy I've ever seen.

It's J.

Mr. Tall, Dark, and Gorgeous blinks at me. "Oh. I think I have the wrong room."

Fully clothed, he's about half a foot taller than me, which makes him average height, with a spare tire and then some around his waist. His eyes glitter brightly behind black plastic hipster frames.

Propping the door open with my hip, I cross my arms over my chest. "Who are you looking for?"

He almost looks like Yoni… but like, ten times hotter. Not that my friend and assistant isn't attractive. He's plenty good-looking.

This guy? Whew.

And he smells good, too. Whatever soap he's using, they should bottle it and sell it.

My face scrunches. Of course they bottle and sell it. It's soap.

He frowns at me. "Is Yoni Aviyente here?"

"He's in the shower."

J looks me over again. His eyes linger on my face, then on my chest, then down in a sweeping gaze more intimate than a caress.

"You're Sadie?"

Nodding, I step back. "I'm guessing you're the brother?"

He nods. "Jared Aviyente. Nice to meet you. Officially."

Holding out his hand, I take it in mine for a shake, and a spark of static electricity runs through my palm. It must be the dry, recycled hotel air.

I jump back. "Come on in."

As I keep the door open, he squeezes past me—and it is a squeeze. I'm definitely plus-sized, and he's slightly thinner than me, but not by much. Mm, I do love me a big boy.

Our children will be fat and cute little cherubs with chunky thighs and arm rolls.

Not that, you know, I actively want kids. I'm just saying.

I want to say something, acknowledge how awkward this is. We've had sex. *Plenty* of sex. He's seen parts of me I don't share with just anyone.

And he's my assistant's brother??

"So you live in town?" I ask Jared as I try to fasten my necklace. The clasp is tiny, and the hook even smaller, and it always gives me fits. My great-aunt gave it to me for my bat mitzvah and thirteenth birthday, so it's always been meaningful to me.

He nods, looking uncomfortable. "Not far from here, actually. Just a few blocks."

"Nice. I like Denver. I haven't been here in a while," I comment. My fingers are clumsy as I try to fix the clasp. "Fuck."

"You okay?" He arches a well-maintained eyebrow.

"I can't get my freaking necklace on," I huff.

He inhales sharply. "You want some help?"

I'm secure enough in who I am—and what I'm capable of —to accept help when I need it.

"If you don't mind."

Jared steps close to me, and I turn my back to him. Holding out the strands of the necklace, his fingers brush mine as they take over the chain, and I move to lift my hair out of the way. I can't get it all, though; I have *a lot* of hair.

The pads of his fingers brush against my neck, smoothing a curl out of his way. A shiver runs through me. One of my biggest turn-ons is someone touching my neck. Specifically, a man's hand across my throat as he fucks into me.

Fuck. Why did I let him help?

He feels solid behind me, steady. I feel like I can trust him.

Which, frankly, is ridiculous. I may be able to trust Yoni, but I've known him for a year. Jared is Yoni's brother, and even though we've gotten naked together, I don't *know* him.

Not yet, at least.

I want to, though. Fuck, do I want to.

The clasp catches, and I know because the necklace chain goes taut against my clavicle before it releases with slack, and I hear his soft exhalation. His thick fingers brush mine again as he takes my hair, and as I let it fall, he finger-combs the curls into place. Heat rises to my face, and I—

"There," he says, his voice rough.

The bathroom door opens, and Jared jumps back.

Yoni has a towel wrapped around his waist, and as he sees his brother—and no doubt how close we're standing—his eyes narrow.

"Hi, Jare. Glad you could make it," he says.

"Thanks for inviting me," Jared says. He clears his throat. "Yonatan, where are your clothes?"

Yoni rolls his eyes. "You're worse than Mom." Crossing the room, he scoops a pair of blue plaid boxers off the bed. "Forgot my undies." He gives his brother a cheeky grin.

"You walk around naked in front of—" Jared huffs. "It's not appropriate."

I roll my eyes. "Well, I'm hardly about to jump him. He's married."

My assistant grins. "Oh, is that the only reason why? We're sharing a room. How do I know you don't have a secret crush on me?"

Jared chokes.

"You know I'd like the power dynamic reversed, honey," I tease.

After spending the day making a thousand decisions, the last thing I want is to take the lead on yet another project. And frankly, sometimes that's what sex feels like: work, a project. Sometimes, I just want to lie there and let someone else do the hard work for a little while so I can mentally recuperate.

Not that I'm an uninterested starfish. I'm just not directing. I like handing over the reins for a bit.

But only when I can trust them. If there's no trust, there's no way they're getting close to me.

"Go get dressed," I tell him fondly. "Then you can taunt me a second time."

As I turn, I realize Jared is still close to me. He backs up quickly, crossing to the bed he's identified as Yoni's.

My bracelet and earrings are on the dresser, and as I put them on, I look Jared over again.

There's definitely a family resemblance. The same deeply tanned skin, dark hair and eyes, and the sharp angle of his nose look just like his younger brother. How did I not notice before this?

"You're older than Yoni?" I ask, squinting at him.

Jared nods. "Four years. I'm thirty-one."

Yoni and I are both twenty-seven; our birthdays are actually a week apart, which is kind of cool.

We actually have a lot in common: same age and friend group, similar upbringings, similar belief systems. Where he's Sephardic, I'm Ashkenazi, but at the end of the day, we're both Jewish, and that commonality does make our working relationship stronger.

"He's awesome. I love him." Flicking my hair over my shoulder, I fasten my earrings. "I'm so glad to have met him."

"You've been friends for a while." Jared narrows his eyes. "Do you prefer Sylvie or Sadie?"

I shrug. "Both. Either. This weekend, I'm Sylvie, but back home, I'm Sadie."

"What's the difference?"

"Sylvie is just an amped-up version of Sadie. More confident, more badass. The kind of person I wish Sadie could be if it wasn't so exhausting."

He tilts his head, studying me. "How is it exhausting?"

"Well, you're a reporter, right?"

Jared nods slowly.

"Are you the same person on air as you are in real life?"

Yoni's mentioned that his brother is an on-air correspondent for the Denver hockey team. He's always traveling, always on the go.

Understanding dawns in his eyes. "No. It's just a more…" He shakes his head. "You're right. It's a more exaggerated version of myself."

"We all compartmentalize. I just happen to name the two parts of myself." I grin. "I swear I don't actually have multiple personalities. They've checked."

He frowns.

Okay, so strike one: he doesn't get my sense of humor.

That's okay. I can roll with the punches. I can still make this work. We can totally fuck this weekend and nobody has to know.

Yoni emerges from the bathroom, dressed now in a pair of dark jeans and crisp button-down shirt with the sleeves rolled up. His curly hair is neatly styled, and as he crosses the room to the nightstand where his watch and wedding ring are waiting, I notice the resemblance between him and his brother even more.

There's another knock on the door, and this time I open it to Lu, wearing a purple velvet jumpsuit with sparkly silver Doc Martens. Her long, blonde hair is pulled back from her face and falls in gentle waves down to her waist.

"Hey, babe," I tell her, propping the door open. "Let me just grab my blazer."

Yoni is already at the closet, handing it to me. "Hi, Lu," he says, as he grabs his leather jacket off the hanger.

"Yoni." She nods, peering behind him. "That's the spouse?"

Jared chokes.

"Nah, that's my brother," Yoni says. "Jared, come meet LuAnn Pierce."

Her eyes flick to me as he joins us at the door, a question in her eyes. I shake my head.

"Nice to meet you," she says, checking him over, then immediately dismissing him. She turns to me. "Your bestie messaged me."

"Which one?" I ask as we head toward the elevator.

"The cute one with the cuter girlfriend."

I roll my eyes. "What did Sullivan want?"

He met Lu at a convention we were all at last year in Reno. We had a great time together. At least, I think we did. The memories are hazy, thanks to enough shots to leave me hungover for three days.

"He thought I'd like to sell one of his sketches with the NSFW graphics on my website," LuAnn says. "He's really good."

The elevator dings, and Yoni and Jared let us board first, the brothers both silent.

"He is." I've tried a few times to get him to draw something for my characters, since I write about hockey and baseball and he's a major sports fan, but he hasn't agreed yet.

"He mentioned his girlfriend is a graphic designer…"

"She's the one who did my new cover," I mention. "The rebrand with the doves?"

"Oh, that was her?"

"Yeah. I'm trying to set her up to do it for me on a permanent basis. She doesn't have to do it full-time, but I want her on my team."

Lu nods. "I'd hire her, no doubt."

"When we're in Nantucket, hopefully she can come to the convention and you can convince her," I suggest. "She needs to be—well, not wined and dined, but plied with orange soda and pasta."

"I can do that," Lu grins.

As the elevator opens on the mezzanine where the happy hour is being held, we head to the bar. The group of women there are antsy for the bartender to finish setting up.

"Sylvie! Lu!"

Friends smile and wave, and a few ladies draw us into a hug. We say hello to the people we know and meet the people we don't.

"What exactly is going to happen?" I hear Jared murmur to his brother.

Yoni grins. "Dude, you're a commodity here. A straight, single man with a full-time job? They're going to love you."

A smile on my lips, I look over at him again. Yoni isn't wrong; Jared has already attracted a fair amount of attention from the group of forty-something women in their thirties and forties.

Since my assistant has been to a few of these before, he's a known quantity. They know he's off limits, even if the shiny band on his left hand didn't proclaim it.

Jared? He's—

A sense of unease rolls up my spine. I don't like the idea of him messing around with one of my friends. I have no claim to him; I just don't like it. I'd feel the same way with—

Well, Sullivan is happily dating Johanna.

Asher's engaged to Arielle.

Elliott is married to Yoni.

Okay, evidently I need to meet more single men.

I don't think it's going to happen at a romance book convention, though.

eight

. . .

Jared

FUCK. Sylvie is *hot*.

Sadie.

Whatever the fuck name she goes by, she is fucking gorgeous.

Her face is pretty, her features romantic, almost poetic. Olive skin, dark eyes, chestnut brown hair falling in gentle waves to frame her face. A single stud in her nose and a ladder of rings up one ear. She's wearing a low-cut gray dress which shows off her killer figure. I want to sink my teeth into the curve of her neck and—

Okay, where did that come from? I'm not a vampire; biting is *not* my kink.

Across the party, she's standing with a group of women about her age, drinking a beer and smiling.

"So what's her deal?" I ask my brother, nodding toward his boss.

Yoni sits back in his seat, smirking at me. "What do you mean?"

"You know what I mean."

"Is she single?" He raises his eyebrows suggestively.

Making a disgruntled noise, I roll my eyes. "Shut up."

I can't deny the fission of heat running through me, though.

"She's single," Yoni finally confirms. "Married to her work, though."

I get that; I'm certainly committed to mine. It's not like I have time for much else these days. I'm always working, either traveling or recuperating from traveling.

My stomach turns at the reminder of the intern. She's doing well; really well. The ratings are always up on nights she broadcasts. I wouldn't put it past the network to take things in a different direction. *Especially* if they can give her a newbie's salary rather than pay for my ten years of experience.

Taking a sip of my gin and tonic, I close my eyes and breathe through my nose. I'm not going to worry about it. Not tonight, at least.

"Tell me about this book convention," I ask my brother.

He shrugs. "Tonight is for the readers to mingle with the authors. Some of them will give readings. Not Sylvie, though. She has her narrator do a performance."

My eyebrow goes up. "She has a narrator?"

"About three quarters of her books are in audiobook format, and we're working on getting the rest of the backlist done," Yoni says proudly. "It should be done within the next six months."

"Nice." I hold my fist out for a bump. I can see how much this means to him. How accomplished this makes him feel.

"Tomorrow, the authors are assigned tables and the readers will come up, buy books, and get them signed. It's more formal, though still fairly laid back. And then tomorrow night, there's a big party. Almost like a Bar Mitzvah party without the kid," he continues.

"So just… a party?"

He grins. "If you say so. There's an open bar and it's— well, it's a lot of fun."

"I'll take your word for it," I mutter as I sip my drink. My eyes flick across the room again.

Sylvie—Sadie—talks animatedly in a group of women. She gesticulates with her hands, including the one holding her beer, and the pretty blonde woman from the elevator laughs uproariously.

"What does she write?" I nod toward her again.

"Hockey romance."

I stare at him. "What?"

"She writes contemporary queer romance novels about a hockey team," he says, like I'm dumb. "She's also written baseball books and a few novels about basketball players."

"People read that stuff?" I can't believe that.

"They go nuts for it."

"Why?"

He shrugs. "Why do people watch hockey on TV?"

"It's a fast-paced game with supremely talented athletes in the prime of their careers," I tell him.

"Okay," he says, waving a hand. "Now add a love story to it."

I blink.

"It's dynamite. Instant sales."

"So she just…"

Yoni raises his eyebrows. "She still has a day job, but between you and me, it's more for the peace of mind than the income. She could totally do this as a full-time gig. She's just not ready to take that leap."

"And you help her?" Even though he's tried to explain it, I've never understood exactly what he does as her assistant.

"I create graphics, monitor ads, administer her shop, update her website, mail out her books, schedule every-thing…" He shrugs. "It's a job, but I like her, and I like being useful."

"You don't want… more?"

He has a biochemistry degree and did a semester and a

half of dental school before dropping out. That was four years ago. Since then, he met and married Elliott, and as happy as I am that my brother's found his forever partner, I can't help wondering if getting off the corporate merry-go-round is holding him back.

Both of our parents are very into education. Our dad is a high school principal and our mother is a dentist. There was never a question of *if* we were going to college; we were going, it was final. The only question was where.

I went to a small liberal arts college in Northern California, and Yoni did undergrad in upstate New York before moving to Boston for dentistry school. After he dropped out, he stayed, rather than going back to Tacoma where our parents live or joining me in Denver.

I mean, I guess I get it. He has a life there. Friends. A partner who is now his spouse.

I wish I could be as happy as he is.

"I like the way things are now," Yoni says. "It works for me. It's not for everyone. It doesn't have to be. It's good for me."

Shaking my head, I meet his eyes. "You're happy, I'm happy. End of story."

"What about you?" My brother tilts his head. "You happy?"

Lifting my gin and tonic to my lips, I sip my drink and think over his innocent question.

"I think I'm about to lose my job," I finally admit.

"Why would you say that? You're a great reporter," he says.

"The winds of change." I shrug. "I like Denver, but I'm not attached to the city. After the season's up, I'll start putting out feelers. See what's out there."

"Come to Boston," he suggests.

I smile tightly. "Yeah, maybe."

"Dude, I mean it." He kicks my foot under the table.

"Even if it's just temporary. Come hang. It'll be great to have you."

"I have to finish the season first."

"There's more to life than work, you know." Yoni rolls his eyes. "I swear, you two are made for each other."

"Who?"

He lifts his eyebrows. "You and Sadie."

My stomach twists. "No. She's your boss."

"So? I'm not sleeping with her."

"And it wouldn't bother you?" I have to check. "If she and I were to…"

"As long as I'm not in the room when you do it, I don't care." He shrugs. "She needs a nice guy. And fuck, buddy, you're a nice guy. You're exactly the kind of guy she needs."

He looks over his shoulder at her, then turns back to me and shakes his head.

"Even if she won't admit it."

nine

. . .

Sadie

WHEN I WAKE UP, it takes a moment to remember where I am. Yoni's snuffling snores in the bed across from mine, though, quickly tell me.

Even though it's ass o'clock in the morning, I start the process of getting ready with a face mask and restyling my obnoxiously flat waves that I wish were curls before sitting at my computer and working on today's project. I finished a book last month and I'm already knee-deep in the next. It never ends. Not that I'd want it to.

I have three weeks to get my next book to Lu for initial feedback and I'm not nearly where I should be with the draft. Just because I *can* crank out 50,000 words in a week doesn't mean I *should*. Or even that I want to.

Self-preservation is not a life skill I possess. Luckily, Yoni keeps me on task.

Sometimes.

Mostly.

He tries, at least. Sometimes my force of will is more effective than his, though.

My character is a happy-go-lucky golden retriever hockey player giving the grumpy equipment manager a blowjob in the locker room. As I try to focus on blond-haired, green-eyed Dane and his hunky enemy-slash-love-interest, though, a different image unravels in my mind's eye.

Instead of the locker room, I see a swanky hotel room. Instead of the equipment manager, I see a husky, hunky guy with dark hair and eyes and a glucose monitor on his arm.

And instead of the hockey player on his knees, it's me.

What is the coincidence that Yoni's brother Jared is the same guy J who fucked me to oblivion—not once, but on two separate occasions?

My assistant talks about his brother all the time. Despite living halfway across the country from one another, he and Jared are close. Much more than I am with any of my sisters—or even all three of them, combined.

Jared kept his distance last night. It makes sense. He was there to see his brother. Not me. *Definitely* not me.

I don't think it was an unpleasant surprise for him, though. It certainly wasn't for me.

Yoni's alarm goes off, shattering my concentration. I've accomplished negative seventeen words today.

Not the best. Certainly not my worst performance of late.

Closing my computer, I continue getting ready for the day ahead. By the time we get downstairs for breakfast an hour later, I'm in an entirely different mindset, and after my coffee and bagel, I'm good to go.

Yoni flutters around me, setting up the table and making sure things are *just right*. This is what he excels at. I don't have the eye for aesthetically-pleasing tablescapes.

Just ask my seventh grade etiquette teacher, Mr. Benjamin. In the multi-purpose room of the local YMCA, he taught our entire class—both boys and girls—how to dance a few basic steps, set a table, arrange a bouquet, navigate formal dining situations, and more. Mostly, what he taught me is the old-fashioned kind of heteronormative etiquette bullshit that I rail against. At the same time, I can admit I need to know the rules in order to break them and declare them toxic as fuck.

Which I do. With great pleasure.

Except for setting the table. I have *very strong opinions* on which side of the plate the fork goes, mainly because my grandmother always insists on putting it in the wrong place. Then again… pretty much everything Myrna does drives me crazy.

Family. Can't live with them, can't live without remembering all the trauma they inflicted.

As if on cue, Yoni's brother appears. To my surprise, he's holding a tray with three coffees.

"Good morning," he says with a roughness to his voice that reminds me of his early morning just-fucked voice. My face heats at the memory of our lazy morning in bed in Boston almost six weeks ago.

Did he get laid last night?

I have no claim on him. So why does the idea of him hooking up with another person bother me?

"Morning," Yoni says. "Thanks for grabbing extra coffee. I haven't had a chance to get away."

Jared holds a cup out to me and swallows. "Do you, ah, need any help?"

He looks like he's afraid I might actually say yes.

What happened to the sexy, strong Soft Dom I met?

As I glance around the table, the boxes of books neatly organized and the banners hung, I can't see anything that needs to be done.

"No, thanks," I say easily. "We're pretty much set."

His gaze narrows on the stack of books on the edge of the table.

"These are your books?"

"Yep." Brightly, I pop the word. "I write queer sports romance novels. I've done baseball, hockey, and I'm moving into basketball next."

His eyebrow goes up. "You write about sports?"

"People go feral for it." His jaw clenches and I smile innocently. "I run a fantasy baseball league for readers, too."

Jared scoffs.

Even though I don't know what his specific problem is, I've been around the block enough to have a few guesses:

He thinks romance isn't "real fiction," which is total bullshit and degrading. Why is it that 99.99% of literature is written by stuffy white men and the same caliber of fiction written by women is downgraded to "women's fiction?" Fuck the patriarchy. If I never read another rambling manifesto by Kerouac or Hemingway, it'll be too damn soon.

He thinks people can't possibly be interested in reading about queer love stories. Maybe not this one—his brother is openly queer, and from all the stories I've heard, he's thoroughly supportive of Yoni.

Or maybe, he thinks I don't know what the hell I'm talking about. Just because he's a sportscaster for Denver's hockey team doesn't mean he's the world's foremost expert on all things sports.

Whatever his problem, I don't have to make it mine.

Lu bustles over. "You good, babe?"

Her face is an inscrutable mask of serenity, the only hint of her anxiety the redness to her eyes. She hands me an airplane bottle of tequila, and as I clink my tiny bottle against the matching one in her hand, we both down the shots.

Warmth floods my system, blurring my senses. Everything is a little easier to process now.

When I nod, she lifts her fists to bump mine.

"We got this," I tell her, and she exhales slowly.

No matter how many of these things I do, they never get easier.

More fun, maybe.

When the doors open, it's time to put on my game face. I

grin at the first reader to approach my table, a woman in her mid-fifties with a sullen teenager behind her.

"OMG, I can't believe I get to meet you!" the woman exclaims. "Nesha—it's Sylvie Hirsch!"

"Nice to meet you." I give her a happy smile. "What's your name?"

"Lisa. I've read all your books. I love…"

We drift into conversation. This is less about sales and more about human connection. But by the time she's done telling me about her favorite of my books, she's decided to take home four paperbacks, too. I'm not mad about that.

Yoni passes me the books and I sign my name with a flourish before he packages them up and adds some swag goodies for her. The teenager's interest is piqued by the acrylic floral bookmarks, and I see him add an extra to the bag for her. She beams, and he winks at her.

He's good at this. He knows how to take care of my readers.

After Lisa moves on, I turn my attention to the next reader patiently waiting her turn. We chat for a few minutes before she purchases a few books, too. And on and on they come.

They don't all buy. Some people need to read the back blurb before they buy, and still more prefer to read on ebook or audiobook. Others aren't interested in my books at all.

That's fine. They're not for everyone. There's a book for every reader and a reader for every book.

Most of my readers are AFAB. The majority of my male readers are queer. Still, there are a few straight men here at the convention, and they tend to gravitate toward my table.

My friend Bethany's dad, a giant biker dude who is the world's biggest Raiders fan, makes his way over. We always have a good time trash-talking the Chargers, a team we mutually hate.

Donovan, one of the models walking around shirtless in a pair of gray joggers, spends fifteen minutes talking to me about the fantasy baseball league I run. He's a good hype man for the events. He looks even better on the cover of my best-selling book, too.

A few of the other guys do double takes when they see my covers and hear their summaries. I'm sure they don't expect to find much ado about sports at an event like this.

Oh, if only they knew…

ten

. . .

Jared

SYLVIE HIRSCH IS A FIRECRACKER. As I watch from a few feet away, she effortlessly charms the pants off nearly every reader to approach her table.

We were only supposed to be here for a little bit. Yoni and I planned to grab lunch or a drink while she was working.

Instead, he's been glued to her side all morning. There hasn't been a moment to pause and get away.

I can't blame him for falling into her orbit. She's like a magnet, effervescent, pulling me in against my will.

She's gorgeous.

I thought she was attractive as S, the mysterious sub from the app who knew exactly the right ways to please me.

I thought she was beautiful as Sadie, my brother's boss who stunned me speechless last night.

As Sylvie, though? She is an absolute fucking knockout.

The worst part is, she knows it.

A pair of men approach the table. They're standing close together, and as they pause in front of her, I watch as one of the guys slides his hand into the other man's back pocket.

"I love the game play in this book," the man on the right

says, tapping on one of the titles. "It makes me feel like I'm back in the dugout with all my friends."

Sadie—Sylvie—beams at him. "Oh, I'm so glad."

"You nailed the pressure and fear of coming out so well," the other dude says. "It's like you saw directly into my soul."

"Thank you." Her smile softens. "That means the world to me."

They talk more as she signs some books for them. When they pass along to the next table, her eyes flick up to mine across the way, and she pauses.

There's a brief lull between readers. Her eyebrows go up, and against my better judgment, I find myself walking toward her.

"Can I get you anything?" I ask. My voice comes out husky, deeper than intended.

She raises her eyebrow at me. "I'm good, thanks."

I want to do things for her. I want to help her. I want to take care of her.

But she doesn't want my help.

"Bathroom break? Water?"

She shakes her head, turning to the next reader with a bright smile.

As much as I know I should walk away, I can't. From across the hotel ballroom, I watch as she greets readers and fans with a cheery smile. I can see what she meant about Sylvie being a more amped-up version of Sadie. She's always smiling, always happy, always "on." She's wearing a mask—entirely different than her submissive persona in the bedroom, and at the same time, so similar, too.

At least when I'm reporting on a game, there's a defined time where I need to be "on" myself. There are clearly delineated points where I can breathe.

Yoni beckons me forward a few hours in.

"You don't have to stand guard," he says. "Thanks for waiting. It's busier than we expected."

"That's good, right?" My brow furrows. There's been a non-stop flow of readers in front of the table. As much as I'd like to spend time with my brother while he's here… well, the view isn't half bad.

He nods. "I'm running out to the lobby to grab our lunch."

"Let me handle it." That's the least I can do.

Now that I think about it, it's been a while since I last ate. Pulling out my phone, I check my glucose monitoring app. Yep—all signs point to it being lunchtime.

"I got you a sandwich and an apple juice, it'll be here in twenty minutes." Yoni gives me a hard look. "Your numbers are good? You look a bit off."

My heart twists. "The juice will help."

His eyes soften. "You need to take care of yourself, Jare."

"I am," I lie.

I should have been the one to buy his lunch; I should be reminding him to eat, not him worrying after me. That's not the way this goes.

He shakes his head. "It's like I have two fucking house-plants now." He doesn't explain, turning on his heel and returning to the table, where there's a crowd of people waiting.

Meeting the delivery person in the lobby, I take the two heavy bags of food. The volunteers at the entrance to the ball-room look suspiciously at my assistant badge before letting me through.

Both of the women check me out. To my surprise, a little shiver runs down my back. They don't look friendly; they look downright hungry.

And where usually that might turn me on… right now, it just makes my balls shrivel up.

Sadie is holding court with another author, readers circled around them and eagerly basking in their attention.

I get it. I'd kind of like to command her attention again, too.

Catching my brother's eye, I heft the bags of food, and he clears a path for me before taking the bag and dividing the contents. I'm left standing there uselessly as the assembled people close in around me, clamoring for a glimmer of her attention.

Sadie doesn't spare a glance for me as a plastic container is set beside her. She continues talking with her readers, gesticulating wildly. Yoni catches her hand, pushing a water cup into it, and she obediently takes a sip before handing it back to him and continuing her conversation.

There's a guy across the aisle with his hands in his pockets. His gaze is trained on Sadie—*Sylvie*. He glances in my direction and I give him an up-nod, which he returns. Who is he? Maybe a boyfriend? It's not like I have a claim on her.

The thought turns my stomach. I don't. She's nothing to me. A one-time hookup. (Okay, two times.) She's my brother's boss.

But she's…

Blowing out a breath, I force myself to walk away and tour the rest of the gigantic ballroom. There are close to a hundred authors here. Some have fairly dense crowds surrounding their tables where others have much more sparse groups.

Those are the tables that draw my attention. Leighton is a bubbly brunette with a Southern drawl, a stack of dark romance books before her. Ashley is a sassy blonde who writes Regency romance. Delilah is a sarcastic librarian covered in tattoos who writes romantic comedies.

When I woke up this morning, I didn't know what any of these genres were, much less the difference between them.

The authors are happy to educate me. It almost reminds me of those book fairs we had in elementary school, where they brought in racks and racks of books to the cafeteria and we were only allowed to pick one or two to take home.

I'm a grown-ass adult, but I also have grown-ass bills, so my wallet won't let me buy more than a few. As I wind my way through the tables, a handful of books call out to me. I'm not shy about purchasing. I have no compunction against reading romance novels. Sure, it might not be something I've done in the past; doesn't mean I can't start now. Clearly they have an allure to them I've never delved into before.

"Who are you here with?" Katja asks as she signs the sapphic high fantasy book I've selected.

"What do you mean?"

She laughs. "We don't see a lot of straight, single men here." She looks me over again. "And no offense, but I'm not getting a queer vibe from you."

That's fair. Although I experimented a few times in college, I quickly figured out that guys didn't do it for me.

Kink, on the other hand? Yeah, that gets me going like nothing else.

Taking care of my partner? Her unwavering trust? Her complete submission? For as long as the scene lasts, I'm happy.

It's only when it's over that I remember how fucking alone I am.

Of course, my mind automatically turns to the last woman I hooked up with—the woman across the ballroom.

"I'm here to support my brother," I tell Katja, which isn't a lie.

She grins, shaking her head. "You single, though?"

Cautiously, I nod.

"Want to grab a drink later?"

A lump gets caught in my throat. "Um…"

My eyes drift over to Sadie—*Sylvie*. She has an unexpected break in readers and she's watching me, a frown marring her gorgeous face.

Katja turns to follow my gaze. "I get it. No hard feelings."

"What do you mean?"

She scoffs. "Fuck, if I had a girl like Sylvie Hirsch in my bed, I wouldn't look elsewhere, either."

"We're not—I don't—"

"Uh huh. Sure." She hands me the book. "So you two haven't…?"

Pressing my lips together, I fix her with a hard look. "I don't know you." Who does she think she is to be privy to the details of my sex life? Of *Sadie's*?

To my surprise, Katja grins again. "That could change."

I shake my head. "I don't think so."

She shrugs, handing me a card with her books printed on them. "If you change your mind."

My mind is already made up. Still, to avoid further confrontation, I take the postcard, tucking it inside the book and mentally moving on.

eleven

. . .

Sadie

EVERYTHING HURTS. My entire body aches, and for one quick second, I almost forget why I put myself through this.

But when I think about the people I met today, the readers I connected with, I know there's absolutely nothing else I'd rather do. Telling stories is my passion. But spending time with the people who love my stories? There's nothing better.

We have a few hours' break to recover from the festivities before tonight's party begins. Cramming a hundred horn-dog authors, an equal number of support staff and spouses, and a few hundred socially awkward readers into a room… then add alcohol to the mix? Yeah, it's bound to be a good time.

Tonight's theme is "Party Like It's 1999" and Andie and Rosemary have gone all out. The attire is formal and I'm wearing a full ballgown—because why the fuck not—with enough strands of pearls that would make a Southern granny approve. I've paired the look with ice-blue eyeshadow, overly arched eyebrows, extra blush on my cheekbones, and I've even crimped my hair.

Let it be known: when it comes to commitment, I'm all in.

Just, well, not romantically. I'm committed to fashion. To work. To friends. To everything except men.

Yoni is wearing a blue velvet tuxedo—because of course he is. His curls are styled effortlessly so, falling into his face like a wannabe greaser.

We're clustered around a small bar table with Lu and Kira, the organizer's daughter. She's too young to drink, so it's up to us to corrupt her in *other* ways. Considering she proofreads the reverse harem erotica her mother writes... not that much left for us to do.

My skin prickles, and I glance over my shoulder casually like that will make me feel better.

It does.

And it doesn't.

Because across the room is Jared Aviyente, his eyes locked on me. He's wearing a dark suit and tie, his thick form filling out the jacket well. His meaty shoulders are deliciously broad.

When our eyes meet, he swallows, and then his chin lifts slightly and his shoulders straighten.

As I watch, he transforms into the sharp, confident Dom I've met twice before. Gone is the nerdy, awkward guy who hovered at my table all day. Gone is the sweet, anxious guy who doted on his brother and took care of me in his own way.

Jared is gone. He's now J, the Dom I met all those months ago.

And I am fucking *ready* for it.

Should I sleep with him? I mean, the sex was hot. Both times, I walked away happy.

On the other hand... he's Yoni's brother. We're connected now in a way we weren't before. I don't even know the laws about sexual harassment of my employee's family members.

Because I can't jeopardize what Yoni and I have.

Yes, Jared—*J*—is hot.

Yes, I enjoyed my time with him.

But he lives here and I'm in Boston. Neither of us want anything more than a night or two. I can't ruin what Yoni and I share for a fling. Because that's all it would ever be.

No, I can't pursue this. I *can't*.

No matter how much I want to.

"Damn," Lu says, turning to look at what's caught my attention. "He cleans up good."

Biting my lip, I have to agree.

But I can't *say* that.

"You know," Yoni says, casually sipping his drink. "He's single."

My eyes flash to his. "What?"

"He's single. You're single," my rat bastard assistant says.

Lu smirks.

"Don't worry, I'm not going to sleep with your brother," I tell him, conveniently ignoring the fact that I already have. If Jared hasn't told him about our hookups, I'm not about to, either.

Yoni shrugs. "You could. I wouldn't care."

"Babe. We're sharing a room." Like that's the real reason why I'm objecting.

"I mean, I don't want to smell the sex fumes. I'll bunk with Lu. We can snuggle," he grins.

My traitorous best friend nods in agreement, pretending like she doesn't absolutely detest cuddling.

"You're something else," I mutter under my breath as I sip my drink.

My skin prickles with awareness, and I feel Jared come up behind me. He doesn't touch me, he doesn't make a sound, but his presence envelops me like a warm blanket fresh from the dryer. He settles between me and my assistant, a reusable water bottle in his hand.

"Hey," Yoni greets his brother. "You want a drink?"

"I'm good, thanks," Jared says. "You look great."

His eyes are on me. I feel the weight of them like the delicious pressure of my weighted blanket when I'm on the verge of a panic attack.

"Thanks," I murmur.

I'm not anxious, though. I mean, not *really*. A tiny bit, yeah, because it's been a long day and I'm overstimulated and worn out. Mostly, though…

I'm trying to think of all the reasons it would be a bad idea to sleep with Jared Aviyente.

Again.

Because let's face it, he's hot, he knows how to use his fucking cock, and he made damn sure I had a good time.

Every—fucking—time.

So…

"Did you have a good time today?" Lu asks Jared.

"Yes. It was… enlightening," he says carefully.

"I saw you talking with Katja," I comment casually. "I didn't take you for a sapphic high fantasy reader."

He shrugs. "I'll try anything at least once."

Katja and I aren't friends, exactly, but we aren't enemies, either. We're just neutral. She's hit on me, I've turned her down, and life goes on. We've done a few promotions together to support both of our books. Our readers don't often overlap, but at the end of the day, queer readers tend to like queer books.

As Jared, Yoni, Kira, and Lu converse around me, I sip my drink and let my mind relax. I've been go-go-go all day, and even though I had a few hours off for a nap, I don't feel rested.

The alcohol helps… for now. Later, I'm going to crash. I might sleep for a week, or at least a solid eight hours.

A few people come up to our table and chat. I've spent the last twenty-four hours talking. My voice is on that scratchy precipice between sexy and hoarse.

"What are your plans for tomorrow?" Jared asks his brother.

"We fly out at noon," Yoni answers. "You have time for brunch?"

He frowns and shakes his head. "I have to be at the studio for pre-game prep. It's a matinee game."

"Shame. Wish I could have spent more time with you."

"Me, too," Jared says quietly.

But for some reason, he isn't looking at his brother.

He's looking at me.

Leighton comes over, bubbly as ever. "Oh my goodness, Sylvie. You didn't tell me you were here with this hunk!" She squeezes Jared's arm, and he winces and shifts away.

"I'm not here with him," I tell her flatly. Leighton is one of the biggest gossips in the industry. I can't tell her anything.

"We're… friends," Jared says awkwardly.

Yoni laughs outright. "He's my big brother, Leigh. He's single and has a full-time job." He raises his eyebrows.

Hers shoot up. "You're shitting me."

"Nope." He pops the P. "One hundred percent single and ready to mingle. Know any women looking?"

Jared looks like he might murder his brother.

I might help him.

It would certainly be justified. Wouldn't it?

"Do you live locally?" Jared asks Leighton, visibly pained.

"Outside Detroit," the Southern transplant says with an exaggerated drawl. "My wife got a job at a research lab out there, and since mine can be done from anywhere…"

"Nice. What kind of research?"

She laughs. "You don't care, honey."

No, but I do. Why is he pursuing this?

He shrugs. "Making conversation."

"Can I talk to you?" Seething, I ask him through gritted teeth.

It isn't a question.

Lu and Yoni exchange a look. I ignore them.

"*Now.*"

Obediently, Jared follows me into the alcove.

"What the hell?" I demand.

He glares at me. "What do you mean?"

"You're being weird," I snap.

"*You're* being weird," he retorts.

The air is thick. Something heavy passes between us.

"What are you doing here?" I don't want him here. He needs to go.

"Spending time with my brother." He sounds so fucking smug. I want to wipe that fucking smirk off his face.

"Because it looks like you're flirting with married women," I spit.

He scoffs. "Wow. Someone sure seems upset by that."

"Leighton is married. She's not interested in you."

Jared shrugs. "Nor me in her."

"So? Don't bother wasting your time."

"I'm not wasting anything," he says easily.

I glare at him.

"You want to get out of here?" He says it like it's so simple. How the hell is he so calm and collected? I'm burning up just being in this close proximity to his thick form.

"I'm not going to sleep with you," I retort.

Even though it's where my mind immediately went.

"Again," he murmurs. His eyes are dark and full of promise.

So maybe his did, too.

A faint smirk curls his lips, and fuck if it doesn't do things to me. White-hot heat runs through me.

"Yeah, *again*. It's not going to happen," I snap.

"Okay," he says agreeably.

"It's not," I repeat.

"Okay," he says again.

"So why are you still here?"

Jared shakes his head, hiding a smile. "You're ridiculous."

"Ex*cuse* me?"

"I said," he says again, stepping closer to me. "You're ridiculous."

"Go to hell."

Instead of fiery, my words come out breathy.

Fuck.

His sharp-sweet scent of eucalyptus and lavender invades my senses, rendering me senseless.

"Only if you come with me, sweetheart," Jared says. His voice is deep, husky. He steps forward, his pointed black dress shoes toe-to-toe with my platform heels.

Even with the help of the four-inch stilettos, the top of my head barely reaches his chin.

His eyes are fixed on mine, his dark brown eyes glowing golden in the dim hallway light.

I'm fixed on his words.

Come with me.

My throat seizes around a swallow.

"Is that a threat?" I ask.

Jared's smirk is deadly—for my panties.

"It's a promise."

twelve

. . .

Jared

SADIE PRACTICALLY THROWS herself at me, her hands clawing at the lapels of my jacket and tugging my body into her. I let her manhandle me—for now—until we're pressed flush together and her mouth is on mine. My hands land on her hips, one sliding around to the small of her back. She grunts and deepens the kiss, slipping her tongue into my mouth.

I wrench myself away.

"Here's how this is going to go," I tell her.

Her eyebrow raises.

"We're going to go back inside. You can have one more drink. Dance a little. And then when the night is over, I'm going to take you upstairs, worship that goddamn gorgeous body of yours, and then fuck you comatose."

Her eyes dilate.

"You good with that?"

She makes a high-pitched keening sound.

"I need consent, babe," I say.

I don't know how it's so easy to slip into the Dom role when sex is on the line, but I can't sustain that confidence without it. When people question my intelligence, when they doubt my capabilities, it's almost like it's a personal failing.

With sex, though, it's easy. There isn't a manual, there isn't one way to do anything, but pleasure is pleasure is pleasure, and what brings me mine is bringing her hers.

"Can't we just go upstairs now?" There's a hitch in her voice, the slightest hint of a whine. Fuck, she falls into the sub role so well.

Pressing a soft kiss to the corner of her mouth, I stroke my thumb across her cheek.

"Later. Enjoy the time with your friends. You don't get to see them often."

Her eyes narrow, clearly confused. "How do you know that?"

"I talk to my brother." I kiss her again. "I know how much this weekend means to you."

"But—"

"Your flight leaves midmorning. We have plenty of time tonight."

Sadie lets out a soft pant, bordering on a whine when I suck on the edge of her jaw. I want to bring her back to my place, really show her a good time, but seeing as we're already in a hotel with plenty of beds…

There's nobody in the dark alcove, but someone could easily open the ballroom doors and come upon us.

Grabbing her hand, I lead her deeper into the crevice of the dark corner. Sadie's eyes are dark on mine when I push her against the wall.

"Where's your head?" I ask as I fall to my knees.

"I've had one drink," she reports immediately. "I had maybe two sips of a second glass."

"You're able to consent?"

She blows out a heavy breath. "Yes. Fuck, yes."

The full skirt of her ballgown floats between us. Slipping

my hands underneath, I set them across her ankles, squeezing gently. She stands upright in a hurry.

"You're going to relax," I tell her, caressing the soft skin at the top of her feet. "I'm going to bring you pleasure. Nobody will know that it's me with my head buried up your dress. Do you understand?"

"Yes," she breathes.

"You're allowed to come," I add. "But only on my tongue."

She squirms. "Sir…"

With my hand on her ankle, I edge her legs apart a bit so I can get between them. I slide my other hand up her leg, teasing, taunting, until I reach the fabric between her legs.

The satin covering her pussy is damp and I breathe in deep, pressing my forehead to her belly over the bodice of her dress. Her rich scent goes straight to my cock, thickening in my suit pants.

"Sir, please," Sadie whispers.

"Please what?" I ask conversationally as my fingers slip beneath the satin.

Her slick skin feels so soft and smooth against my fingertips, and I release her ankle to press the heel of my hand against my dick. This isn't about me. It's about her. It's always about her.

This is what gets me going like nothing else. My entire world narrows to focus on her pleasure. That's the only thing that matters: making her come as many times as possible.

And given our two nights together… yeah, I'm learning what she needs.

Ducking my head beneath her skirt, I pull her panties to the side and dive in, licking at her smooth flesh. Sadie gasps out loud at the first touch of my tongue to her skin.

She tastes even better than I remember, the rich musk flooding my mouth and overriding my senses. There's nothing I love more than the taste of a woman, her soft pants and moans as I bring her to the brink.

My fingertips caress her legs and thick thighs as she quivers above me. The fabric of her dress falls down my back, half-covering me.

If anyone were to happen upon us, there's no denying what we're getting up to.

And even though I don't have an exhibitionism kink, the thought that someone might catch us like this has my blood boiling.

I suck and lick at her sweet folds and am rewarded with the most beautiful pant. My fingers slide through her slickness, opening her up further for me. Sadie adjusts her stance, widening her legs and letting me in.

Sliding a finger inside her, I devour her shiver and allow her to acclimate before I pull back and thrust back in. When she's ready, I add a second finger and crook them, searching for that spot where—

She groans, long and loud, and I smirk against her pussy, thrusting against the place that makes her shake above me.

Her hand falls to my fabric-covered head, pressing me closer to her. There's no better way to die than with a woman's thighs smothering my face.

But there will be time to enjoy this later. Right now, it's got to be quick and dirty. I lick at her with purpose, my fingers thrusting fast and ruthless.

In a matter of minutes, she's crying out, her pussy spasming around my fingers. I don't relent, sucking at her slick skin until every last drop of her pleasure is mine.

Only then do I withdraw from beneath her dress, bringing my fingers to my mouth to suck them clean.

Sadie lets out a feeble moan, leaning against the wall like she'd collapse without it there behind her.

My eyes on hers, I adjust her panties to cover her pussy, then fluff the skirt of her full ballgown around her.

"Feeling better?" I ask casually as I rise to my feet, dusting off my pants.

Her pulse thunders in her neck. "I—you—*fuck.*"

"Is that an offer?" I ask mildly.

"Yes? No?"

She squeezes her eyes shut and covers her forehead with the back of her hand, like she's trying to hide but can't quite manage it.

"I don't like you," she finally says.

Barely, I manage to hold back my scoff. "Noted."

Her brain might dislike me, but her body clearly does.

"This doesn't mean anything," she says.

I roll my eyes. "Yeah. Okay."

"It doesn't," she insists.

"Okay. Then I'm going to go back to the party."

Her eyes flit down to where my pants are tented, like an obscene archer's arrow, pointing directly at her. "Like that?"

"I'm sure I can find someone to help take care of my needs," I say casually.

I have absolutely no intention of doing so. If she doesn't want to do this again, fine, great, I can take care of it myself.

If she wants another round…

She grimaces. "Why are you so fucking good at that?"

"Do you really want to know?" I ask mildly. "Or would you rather I show you again?"

She swallows.

I need to regain the upper hand—quick.

"Head on up to the room," I tell her, my voice hoarse and husky.

Sadie smirks up at me.

"I expect you to be on your hands and knees, naked and waiting for me." My cock jerks at the idea and I swallow the lust threatening to boil over in my veins.

"And if I'm not?"

She is such a brat, and fuck if I don't enjoy it.

"Then your ass will meet my hand. Several times, in fact."

Fuck, I'd love to give her a good spanking. I almost hope she disobeys.

Her pupils dilate even further. "And if I want that?"

My eyes pin hers. "Are you a good girl?" I run my tongue over my lips, relishing every last taste of her. "Or do you need to be punished?"

I graze my teeth over her earlobe and am rewarded with her hitch of breath.

"You tell me, sweetheart."

However she wants to play this, I'm down. As much as I prefer pleasuring her, I'm perfectly happy to enact punishment. The last two times together have proven we get along like fireworks. She knows just what to say and do to bring me to the edge.

"I'm a good girl," she says softly, her eyes on the floor.

But she doesn't sound certain.

"Are you sure?" My voice is as rough as gravel, my cock hard as steel, my zipper biting an indentation along the length.

Fuck, the things I want to do to her...

"I'm a good girl," Sadie says more firmly. She steps forward and her hand cups my cock, squeezing my hard length over my pants.

Wrenching her hand away, I pin it behind her back, then grab her other arm, leaving her trapped in my hands' shackles. The angle forces her chest out, and I lean down to bite roughly against the point of her nipple.

"Only good girls get my cock."

The words come out automatically and she arches against me. She cries out, thrusting her chest forward.

"Please, sir."

"I don't think you're a very good girl right now," I tell her seriously, before I release one hand. Her arms stay crossed behind her back.

As I pinch and pluck at her breast, her mouth falls open, her gasps the most beautiful sound I've ever heard.

"I'm a good girl," she repeats. "Please, sir."

I meet her lips for a bruising kiss, my tongue plunging into her mouth.

She may be submissive in this role, but she isn't a passive sunflower. She gives as good as she gets, meeting me eagerly.

When I palm her breast, massaging the firm swell over the bodice of her dress, she gasps again.

"Can you be quiet, good girl?" I graze her nipple with my teeth again and am gifted with the softest pant.

"I can be quiet, Sir. I can do it for you." Her voice is breathy, her pupils dilated, her mouth parted.

I trace her lips with my fingers, and she automatically sucks my thumb into her mouth, swirling her tongue around me.

Bringing my mouth to her ear, I demand:

"Prove it."

thirteen

. . .

Sadie

ARIELLE TAKES one look at me and grins.

"Someone got *laid*," she sings out.

"Fuck you," I tell her with an exasperated smile.

"Nah. Seems like you already did."

I press my lips together. "Well, for those of us who don't have our own personal pleasure humans at our beck and call…"

She rolls her eyes. "First of all, gross. Second of all, I love that you call Asher that."

Her fiancé is a giant teddy bear. They were childhood friends, having feelings for each other over the years but never quite connecting until last Chanukah. Now, they're planning a wedding.

I'm the flower girl. I wanted to be maid of honor, but I can concede that their shared best friend from childhood, Estee, is probably a better bet. Especially since Yoni will be the best man. Besides, I kind of like the idea of flinging flowers at people. It won't be a dainty toss-toss like Galinda teaching Elphaba how to whip that hair back and forth. I'm going to lob those fuckers like softballs.

Arielle sets her hand on my arm and smiles. "I'm happy for you. Are you going to see him again?"

"I don't think so."

"Okay." She accepts this easily. "I'm glad you got laid."

"Me, too." I laugh. "It had been a while."

A woman down the aisle looks over at us, eyebrows raised.

Arielle sputters out a laugh. "Come on," she says, pushing the cart forward.

We're grocery shopping together. The local Costco isn't quite so local; it's a trek to get out to Everett each month, and then transporting our supplies home.

We started doing this when we lived together, acquiring the household supplies. Now that we aren't constantly on top of each other anymore, it's a way for us to get together when everything in life gets crazy. Rachel sometimes joins us, but since Erik's family is in town this week, she's busy with them.

We shop and catch up. Arielle's gearing up for the busy season—she works for the Boston baseball team in their social media department and travels to every other road game, sometimes gone for a week at a time. Asher is a teacher and his spring break lines up with spring training, so they took a nice working week down to Florida together. It's a good thing he's a baseball fan.

When I was writing baseball books, she got me access to the clubhouse and I was able to interview players for background research. It was insanely helpful to have a friend in the industry. Now, I'm writing hockey, and lucky for me, Vanessa works for the Boston Grizzlies *and* her boyfriend Sven plays for the team.

I went to my fair share of hockey games this season. Like every other Boston resident, I'm hoping they go far into the playoffs—2011 was *way* too long ago!—and I'm attending now partly for research and partly because I genuinely love the team.

Also, between Vanessa's employee perks and Ceci's… *Ceciness*, I can usually get in for free, so it's easy to justify paying $25 for a single beer.

Next up, I have basketball books on my radar. I don't know anyone involved in the Boston basketball world…

… yet.

"What are you doing next weekend?" Arielle asks as we make our way through the bakery.

"Work." Most weekends I'm at the bookstore. It makes more sense to be there during our busiest times, plus it lets my staff take some weekend days off.

She rolls her eyes. "For Passover, you dolt."

"Oh. Who's doing the Seder this year? You're not going home."

She shakes her head. "Nope. We're low contact with his parents, my parents are being dicks, and, well…"

"You want to go to Bubbie Ruth's?"

The Jewish deli doesn't host a Seder, per se, but it does offer a very nice brisket dinner with matzo ball soup. And pickles. Can't forget the half-sour pickles.

"Elliott and Yoni are hosting a non-traditional Seder," Arielle continues.

My eyebrows go up.

Both Arielle and I grew up in Conservative households, where Elliott's family was Modern Orthodox. In recent years, they've backed away from the traditional side of things. That they even want to host a Seder is strange enough.

"I think we're all kind of missing the culture, even if the religious aspects may not be what we're believing these days," Arielle finally says. Stopping in front of the meat counter, she pulls an enormous slab of meat into the cart. "Yoni already promised to make his Saba's brisket."

"The famous brisket?"

I've heard about Yoni's grandfather's brisket over the years. Sephardic culture is rich in Middle Eastern traditions, whereas my Ashkenazi upbringing more closely follows Eastern European traditions. Even though we're both Jewish, the traditions are very different, and so is the food.

Sephardic foods involve a lot of spices, fruits like dates and figs, and aromatics like leeks and scallions.

And Yoni's grandfather's brisket? He uses apricots and figs to flavor the meat instead of the Ashkenazi version of corn syrup or sugar. They also eat *kitniyot*, rice and legumes, which are prohibited during the week of Passover in my family's traditions.

Whereas my family came from Poland, Romania, and Ukraine, Yoni and Jared's family was originally from Spain; after the expulsion, they moved to Morocco and then Greece before settling in Israel. When their father was a child, the family moved to the States for his grandmother's job with the Israeli embassy, and that was it.

"So you're going to Yoni and El's?" I ask casually.

Arielle nods, hefting a 5-pound bag of onions into the cart. "I'm sure you can come, too."

"Oh, I don't want to impose."

My best friend stops in her tracks and stares at me.

"What? Do I have something in my teeth?" I move my hand to cover my mouth.

"You don't want to *impose*?" She repeats incredulously. "Who are you and what have you done with Sadie Hershkowitz?"

I shrug. "I just…"

"Tell me you didn't sleep with Yoni," Arielle demands quietly.

My eyebrows go up. "What? He's married."

She blinks at me.

"Oh, and gay," I add in. "Still—no. He's my assistant."

"So why do you twitch every time I say his name?"

Because I slept with his brother.

Three times.

Four, if I include the hallway.

Fifteen, if I include all the times I've replayed the memories in my head this week.

"Is he not working out as your assistant? Do you need distance in the friendship?" Arielle asks as she loads the cart with ten pounds each of sweet and regular potatoes. For a sprightly little thing, she sure is strong.

"It's fine. He's great." I sigh. "I'm just in a little bit of a funk."

She nods in understanding. "Post-signing blues?"

"Yeah. It was a great weekend."

"Because you got *laid*." She waggles her eyebrows.

"I was hoping you'd forget about that," I mutter, putting more vegetables into the cart.

"Why? It's not like you've ever been quiet about it in the past."

That's true. I might not brag, but I definitely don't have that shameful attitude about sex. I'm single and having fun. I'm not hurting anyone.

But Jared and I? That can't happen again. The six degrees of Kevin Bacon are too close.

Then again... he lives in Denver. I live in Boston. It's not like we're suddenly going to be running into each other all the time.

fourteen

. . .

Jared

THIS FUCKING INTERN.

"I don't know what happened, Jared," the twenty-year-old kid says with big, round eyes. "The prompter must have failed."

Yeah, no shit, Sherlock. The only way my entire segment's prompt copy should have failed was if the text file was *deleted*.

Once I upload my text to the server, it's his job to feed it into the teleprompter so I can see it on air. Instead, I got to ad-lib an entire segment and then cut to commercial early, which costs the station money.

"Aviyente," my boss calls from across the floor. "A word."

This is the third time Todd the intern has messed up and it's directly impacted me—in the last three weeks. My role does not include supervising him, nor does it involve any sort of management or mentoring.

But for the third time in three weeks, I'm getting reamed for something he did. I'm a lucky scapegoat. I've been in this role for a few years and I'm due for a raise. Or I would be, if the intern didn't keep messing up my segment, making me look like a fool on air.

Gen has her I Mean Business face on, which means nothing good is going to happen.

And as I sit there, letting her detail the myriad ways in which I've fucked up over the last six months, I feel my soul shrivel up and die inside of me.

I don't need to be berated. I fucked up my broadcast by ad-libbing through it. I know it. She doesn't have to tell me fifteen different ways; once was enough, twice is plenty.

I've been doing this long enough to read the writing on the wall.

So when she reams into me… I check out.

"I think it's best if we part ways," Gen says.

"Do you want this to happen now, or at the end of the season?" I ask mildly.

It's the end of March, but Denver's season is pretty much done in the next four weeks, anyway. There's not a snowball's chance in Arizona that they can win every single one of the seventeen remaining games to make it into playoff contention. Gretzky, Datsyuk, Orr, Crosby, AND Bergeron combined couldn't do it. Denver? They don't stand a chance.

Gen glares at me. "I think we're done here," she says. "HR will be in touch."

She presses a button on the phone. "Can I get security up here, please?"

Ten minutes later, I'm escorted out of the building and my press pass is revoked.

I don't know what to do. Do I just… go home?

I want to get drunk. I want to completely eat until my face goes numb and my stomach hurts and I forget about everything.

But if I were to do that, I'd probably end up in the hospital in a diabetic coma, so…

Not going to happen. Not today, at least.

Instead, I check my glucose reader on my phone.

My numbers aren't bad. I can probably tolerate a greasy

burger and fries, just not the milkshake I'd like to go with them.

I look at the numbers again.

Okay, I should probably try a chicken sandwich instead of the burger.

Hitting up the drive-through, I send my brother a text. *Called it.*

He sends back a question mark.

That offer for your couch still available?

My phone starts to ring.

"What happened?" Yoni asks, sounding so much like our mother I shiver.

"Got fired," I tell him flatly, like taking the emotion out of the two words will magically extract all of the feelings from within me. Hey, it works for some men, so even though it's never actually worked for me, maybe this time will be the charm.

"Jare…"

The concern in the single syllable of my brother's voice does me in.

"I don't know what I'm going to do," I tell him honestly. "I was glib about it before. I thought I'd at least have time to look for a new job. Maybe resign on my own terms."

"How much do you have saved up? Enough to make it through?"

I think about my account balances. "A few months, maybe. Depends how much COBRA costs. And my therapist isn't covered by my insurance, anyways…" Living with diabetes means I can't go without health insurance. Aside from the cost of insulin pumps and replacing my CGM, I can't run the risk of a serious side effect happening.

Yoni murmurs something on the other end. A deep voice sounds like Elliott.

"Come here," my brother says.

"I don't have the funds for a vacation, Yo-yo."

I can practically hear his eye-roll. "I have a spare room."

"It's my job to take care of you, not you take care of me," I point out, trying to hide my instinct to pout.

"Jared. We're adults," Yoni says.

"So?"

"So little brother, big brother… none of that matters. We're just brothers," he says. "I'll take care of you, you'll take care of me. You don't have to always be the strong one. It's okay if you lean on me. Fuck, I've been leaning on you my entire life."

"I know. That's why I need to—"

"That's why you need to let me take a turn, too," he says firmly. "Just because you're older doesn't mean it all falls on you. You're not my parent. You're my brother."

"I want to take care of you. That's my job," I tell him quietly. It always has been. Since the day my parents brought him home from the hospital and told me to look out for my baby brother, I've done so.

"It might have been back then." Yoni scoffs. "I'm fully capable. I want us to be equals. Peers. I'm not yours to take care of."

I fall quiet, letting his words filter through my brain.

"Put your stuff in storage and come here," he says firmly. "Your lease is up next month anyway. You'll stay with us until we can find you a spare room. I think Ash might be able to lend his."

"I can't ask that of your friend."

"You're not," he snaps. "I am. He's my friend, you're my brother. It's not an issue."

"Yo-yo…"

"Jare, I'd move heaven and earth for you," my little brother says quietly. "After Elliott, you're my favorite person in the world. Fuck, we could probably get you a job, too. Arielle works in baseball, and Sadie's friend works for the Boston hockey team. We'll figure something out."

"I can't…"

"You can and you will," Yoni declares. "Shut up and do what I say."

"When'd you get so bossy?" I mumble, even though I already know I'll go along with his insanity.

"Shut up and take it." I can practically hear his grin.

"That's my line," I sass back, more out of habit than actual good humor.

"Hey, as long as she consents, I don't care what she says," he says.

The line is silent with static for a few moments.

"Thanks, Yo-yo," I tell him quietly.

"We're family. I'll always be your soft place to land."

———

I arrive in Boston with two suitcases, a backpack, and one hell of a junk-food hangover. After a three-day binge, my sugar is majorly out of whack. I think I can hear colors and smell sounds.

Yoni picks me up at baggage claim and immediately wraps me into a hug. Not a perfunctory man hug; this is a solid hug, arms wrapped around me, holding me tight.

"I'm sorry, Jare," he says quietly. "But I'm glad you're here."

Inhaling sharply, I let the tension coiling within me release.

"Me, too, Yo-yo," I admit. Getting fired fucking sucks.

My brother slaps my back. "Come on. Let's get out of here."

Outside, we hail a ride-share and zoom toward the other side of the city.

"Gotta make a stop on the way," Yoni mentions when the car pulls up outside a shawarma shop.

"What's here?"

He knows I don't like shawarma. It was pretty much the only thing I ate on my 14-day Birthright trip to Israel in college, and now just the sight of it makes me queasy.

"This is Sadie HQ," Yoni says. "My computer was running an update so I couldn't grab it before I left. There's some admin I have to do tonight."

Up a flight of stairs, he punches a code into the keypad and lets himself in.

Inside, the apartment is bright and airy. There are plants on the windowsill and portraits of flowers on the wall.

I swallow. "Is she here?" My heart is pounding at the thought of seeing her again, of being in her private space without her knowing.

"Nah, she's at the bookstore," he answers.

My stomach drops. Why am I so disappointed by that? Of course she's not here. She has her own life.

I haven't talked to her since I left her naked in her hotel room bed three weeks ago. Why would I? I don't have her phone number and we aren't friends. So we've hooked up a few times. It was fun. Great while it lasted. But it doesn't need to happen again.

Especially now that I'm here, taking advantage of my brother's generosity.

I don't know why I suggested we keep in touch. The way she blew me off… I should have known I was reading too much into the situation. I always do.

He disappears into a back room. I hear him rummaging around for a few moments before he returns with a laptop in his hand. "All set. Hey, you want to grab dinner downstairs before we head out?"

I glare at him.

Yoni smirks. "Yeah, I thought so."

Cuffing him gently behind the head, I hurry down the stairs again, his laughter echoing in the stairwell behind me.

His apartment is only a few stops away on the T. Inside, Elliott is at the stove, stirring something that smells delicious.

"Hey, Jared," Elliott says. "Good to see you."

"You, too." I let them pull me in for a hug. "It's been a while."

Elliott gives me a small smile. "Well, we're fixing that now. How're you holding up?"

My heavy sigh seems to be answer enough, because their smile drops and they nod.

"Yeah. I get that."

Elliott and I are more alike than I am to my brother half the time. El identifies themselves by the work they do, much like I do—*did*. Whereas Yoni is happy with his assistant role and has other ways to find fulfillment in his life, El and I don't operate that way.

"I made potato leek soup and I just put the chicken in the oven," Elliott comments. "The sheets are changed in the spare room. You can stay as long as you need to."

A lump forms in my throat. El uses the room primarily as their office on the days they don't go into the lab.

"I'll be out of your hair soon," I promise.

Elliott squeezes my shoulder. "Okay. Soon can be relative. We're not rushing you."

"Why don't you get settled," Yoni says softly. "Take some time to process."

Following him to the spare room, I deposit my suitcases and crash onto the bed. I'm mentally and physically exhausted.

Everything hurts. It's more than a physical ache—it's existential, too. What am I going to do next? I can't stay in my little brother's spare room forever.

fifteen

. . .

Sadie

"OKAY, BUT, LIKE," Ceci says, her wine glass tipping precariously. "How was it?" She raises her eyebrows suggestively.

The Neurospicy Book Club meets monthly in the back of the bookstore I manage. Our core group of people is highly active and our attendance grows each month.

Kiley had a date last week with her dad's best friend and business partner. We were all surprised when the 20-year old told us she had a date with the 35-year old, especially considering she hasn't *dated* much. He didn't know her growing up; they only met once she was an adult, so it was easier for us "older sisters" to approve of the situation. We don't want her to be taken advantage of.

Kiley covers her face with her hands, but she can't hide her blush.

"That good?" Ceci pushes. "Or that bad?"

"Let's rephrase," Bex cuts in. "Would you sleep with him again?"

"Yes," Kiley says without hesitation, and the room erupts in cheers.

The book club started as a fun thing to do. Arielle, Rachel, and I wanted to talk about our love for romance novels. I convinced the previous store manager to let us host it in the bookstore, put out a few flyers... and thirty people showed up.

Ceci is eccentrically fabulous. Bex is working on her Ph.D. in biostatistics and Vanessa works for the Boston Grizzlies Hockey Club; they played lacrosse together at Michigan. They live with Elsy, who is a top violinist with the Boston symphony. Johanna is dating my bud Sullivan—he came into the store looking for a book club for her, but he became one of my closest friends along the way. Rory works with Sullivan's brother-in-law as a personal trainer at their hoity-toity one-percenters gym. Viv and Kate are rugby players—like, legit rugby stars, on the US National team, and Viv's been to the Olympics *twice*. She is seriously intimidating.

And I can't forget Madison, our lone male representative. He's a romance writer like me. We met at a writing group meet-up a few years ago and he's been a barnacle stuck to my side ever since.

Well. Since his parents died, leaving him to raise his five younger siblings, he's been a little less barnacle-y. He's got a lot going on. We all get that his priorities have shifted.

Each month, we hang out in the back of the store, drink wine and eat snacks, and talk about books. It's a safe place for us to unwind and be ourselves. These people are my friends, my family. They get me in a way my parents and sisters never could.

I have my author friends, too. They're part of my community. There's a whole network of people like me in the industry and I've spent the better part of five years immersed in it.

The meeting isn't formal. We talk across the circle about books, but there's no required reading each month. It's more of a hangout section in our favorite place than anything organized with structure and rules.

Rachel corners me around the snack table. "What's up with you?"

"Nothing's up," I tell her automatically.

She narrows her eyes. "You haven't talked about your book signing last month. Like, at all. Did something happen?"

I shrug. "It was fine."

"Lu wasn't a menace?"

"Lu is always a menace." I laugh. LuAnn has visited Boston twice in the past few years, and both times I've brought her to book club. She would fit in perfectly here if she didn't live in North freaking Dakota.

"I'm just worried about you," Rachel says, squeezing my arm. "We don't hang out much anymore."

I bite the inside of my cheek.

We used to live together, us and Arielle. Then Ari started dating Asher and he essentially moved into our apartment. When our lease was up last fall, we all went our separate ways: I bought my townhouse, Rachel moved in with her long-term boyfriend, and Ash and Arielle found a place for themselves.

I do miss that apartment, though.

"We'll grab dinner soon," I promise Rach. "You, me, and Erik."

She shrugs. "Yeah, sure."

Squinting at her, I try to figure out why she sounds so noncommittal about something that was essentially *her* idea.

"Everything good with you two?"

Rachel hums. "I don't really want to get into it."

My eyebrows go up. "That means it's *not* good."

"I just—" She sighs. "Can we do brunch after Passover is over? You, me, mimosas, maybe some blitzes from Bubbie Ruth's?"

"Just like old times." I squeeze her arm. "You got it, babe. Boozy brunch, no boys allowed."

Pulling out my phone, we compare calendars, finding a date that works for us both.

See? This is what's great about being single. I don't need to check in with anyone. I can just do things.

Jared's soft request flits through my brain. *We can keep doing this. It doesn't have to end.*

It does, though. It did. For both of our sakes.

My invitation to the Seder didn't get lost in the mail—Yoni simply added it to my online calendar, like it was fait accompli that I'd be there.

And really, it's not like there's anywhere else I'd be. I can't fathom the thought of working at the bookstore during the Seder. It's antithetical to everything I was raised to do. Sure, I may not believe or observe all the traditions, but some are ingrained so deeply I couldn't pry them out of my soul with a crowbar.

So I put on a nice outfit, did my hair, and stopped by the store for a few bottles of Kosher for Passover wine. Knocking on Yoni and Elliott's door, I'm surprised when it swings open immediately.

And then my insides go haywire.

Because it's not my assistant standing there. It's his brother.

"What are you doing here?" I blurt.

He looks as good as ever. His dark curls are rich and luxurious and his beard is neatly trimmed. He's wearing a dark green dress shirt, the sleeves rolled up his forearms, and dark jeans that do wonders for his thick form.

Jared wrinkles his forehead. "I… live here."

"Here?" My voice comes out in a squeak.

"Temporarily," he sighs. "I—well, I had to come to Boston for a while."

My eyebrows go up. "Look, dude… I know we had a good time, but, like—"

He snorts. "Nothing to do with you. It's more I had to leave Denver."

"Ah."

"So I'm staying with Yo and El until I can find a new job," he says with a casual shrug of his shoulders. "Do you want to come in?"

Swallowing my hesitation, I nod, and he steps aside to let me pass.

He takes my coat without comment, but I can feel the way his eyes burn into me when my simple shift dress is revealed. It's a soft green fabric with darker green and yellow flowers embroidered.

We match.

"You look nice," he murmurs, his voice dropping an octave.

"Thanks." Without ceremony, I hand him the bag of wine. "Here, make yourself useful."

Jared snorts and shakes his head, turning down the small hallway.

"Sadie! You made it!" Asher Gold gives me a giant grin from the small den area.

Crossing the room, the giant teddy bear gives me an enormous hug, lifting me clear off my feet. And that's no easy feat. We're both several dozen pounds above a healthy weight.

"How've you been, Ash?"

"Doing well." He gives me a poke in the side. "You been a good girl?"

"Always," I tease back.

But the word has a different meaning with Jared here. I'm his *good girl*.

Not right now, though. For now, I'm just me and he's just him and we just exist in this place. We're not in a scene. We're essentially strangers.

Asher settles back into his seat beside Arielle. I say hello to the others—Alex and Mara, Rachel and Erik, and some other mutual friends.

Am I the only single one here?

No. Jared's here, too.

Fuck. Is this a set-up?

sixteen

. . .

Jared

I **FIND** my brother in the kitchen.

"Hey, Jare," Yoni says. He hands me a giant bowl of salad. "Can you put this on the table?"

"What's she doing here?" I ask instead.

He raises an eyebrow. "Who?"

"Sadie."

"Uh… she's my friend?" He looks confused. "Oh, and technically my boss, too, if you want to be pedantic about it."

"Yeah. So why is she here for the Seder?"

He stares at me. "Because she's my friend?"

I gape back at him.

"Look, I know you have a hard-on for her or something, but—"

I splutter. "I don't."

Yoni raises his eyebrows. "Please. You guys totally hooked up."

"She *told* you?"

"No. You did," he says, like I'm the dumbest person on the planet.

"I don't kiss and tell," I snap.

"Except you just did," he sing-songs. "Also, you disappeared in the middle of that party, never came back, and the hotel door was dead-bolted. She had bite marks all over her neck the next day. More than I needed to know, dude." He shakes his head. "Yeah, if the two of you didn't hook up, she slept with someone. And the only one she had eyes for that weekend was you."

I look around the small apartment. She's only a few feet away, a glass of wine in her hand as she chats with some of the other guests. "I'm not talking about this right now."

"Oh, but we definitely will later," my little brother says with a broad smirk.

He's such a little shit.

There are six couples here for dinner, not including me and Sadie. I knew my brother and his friends were all settling down, but I didn't realize I was one of the last dinosaurs that hadn't coupled up.

So much of my life the last few years has been work, work, work. Being on the road for 82 games a year takes a toll on personal relationships. Hell, the Denver hockey team has a game tonight. Even though I typically ask for all of the Jewish holidays off from my employers, it's not like I have anyone to share and celebrate them with once I leave the arena or the studio.

My sour mood takes a turn for the worse when Sadie is seated beside me at the dinner table. She's engaged in conversation with Arielle and Mara, as radiant as ever. Her star shines brightly no matter where she is. I kind of hate her for that.

When I'm on camera, I can be professional. Enthusiastic, even, when it comes to analyzing plays and statistics.

Outside of that?

I'm floundering like a goldfish plucked out of its bowl, left for dead on the side of the road.

Who am I without work? What do I do now?

Sadie virtually ignores me during the quick service—Yoni

and Elliott prefer a non-denominational, non-traditional retelling of the Passover story—and all through the ritual meal. Aside from a brief "pass the potato kugel," she doesn't talk to me at all.

I don't like that.

But I also don't know how to change that, how to catch her attention.

We've hooked up three times. Now I'm in Boston for the semi-permanent future, but I have nothing to offer her. No job, no apartment, no prospects. All I have to offer is sex.

Is that enough for her?

I'd like to see her again, to bury my face in her pussy and make her scream until she cries. I'd love to try all sorts of new things with her. She's so fucking responsive. In our short time together, her body was attuned to mine. I can't imagine how explosive we'd be if we actually took the time to get to know each other.

After the dinner dishes have been cleared and we've all recited the Birkat HaMazon and the million verses of Chad Gadya, Sadie disappears down the hallway to the bathroom. She's more than a little tipsy, having consumed almost an entire bottle of wine over the last three hours.

To my surprise, it's less than thirty seconds later that my phone buzzes in my pocket.

New match in your area, reports my kink app.

Swiping open the app, I'm surprised when Sadie's profile pops up. She's looking to get laid right now? There's no way she's sober enough to consent. Anyone who she meets up with would be out of line to pursue anything.

Before I can stop myself, I send her a message.

What are you doing, little girl?

Fuck off.

Shaking my head, I turn down the hallway to the bathroom.

You okay?

She doesn't respond.

The toilet flushes and the sink runs, and a minute later, the door opens. She's not looking where she's going and crashes directly into my chest.

My hands go to her hips, steadying her.

"Are you okay?" I ask her quietly.

"What, are you fucking stalking me now?" she snaps.

"I just want to make sure you're okay. You're not in a headspace to consent."

Sadie's eyes flash. "What, you think I'm going to sleep with you?"

My laugh is cold. "No, but will whoever you meet up with from the app make sure you're good, or will they just fuck you and move on?"

"Maybe that's what I want," she says, her voice a challenge.

"Is it really?" My tone is mild.

"I—you—ugh." She scrubs at her face. "Why are you even here?"

"I told you. I'm staying with my brother until I find a job." Even if it does make my insides twist.

"No. Here. Outside the bathroom." She raises her eyebrows. "Stalker, much?"

"I wanted to check on you, make sure you were good."

She rolls her eyes. "We're not in a scene anymore. You don't own me."

"What if I want to?" The words come out automatically.

Sadie blinks a few times.

"Look, it doesn't have to mean anything," I hurry to add. "We had a good time together, didn't we?"

Slowly, guarded, she nods.

"It doesn't have to be anything more than it's been the last few times."

She chews her cheek, deliberating. "I'm not fucking you in Yoni's house," she finally says.

I shudder. "Hell no. I—no. Not here."

"So I guess you're going to have to escort me home. Since I'm clearly too drunk to safely be in a ride-share all by myself." Her eyes are bright—tipsy, yes, but not drunk.

"I can do that," I tell her carefully. My cock chubs up in my pants, already anticipating what will happen next.

"Let's make this clear," Sadie says firmly. "This thing—we don't tell anyone. It doesn't mean anything. And for fuck's sake, it can't happen again."

"You've got a deal."

seventeen

. . .

Sadie

"FUCK MY FUCKING LIFE!" Angrily, I smash my hands against the keyboard, hoping it will magically form words.

"Okay, babe, you need a break," Yoni says calmly.

"I'm *fine*," I tell him.

From across the room, he rolls his eyes. "Do you want to talk through the scene? Or do you want to go for a walk?"

"How about you jump off a cliff and fucking die?" I mutter without looking up from my computer's monitor.

Why won't this locker room rimming scene work? The characters are primed and ready to go, but everything I type comes out pedantic and *boring*. Definitely not sexy.

His eyebrows go up. "Okay, so you definitely need to eat something. You can't survive just on coffee and spite."

"Watch me."

With a controlled sigh, Yoni gets up from his desk and walks to the mini fridge in the corner. Door open, he stops and stares.

"Fuck."

"What?" I look over at his sad face and feel a twinge of emotion for a microsecond before I return to my pity party.

"I forgot my lunch at home," he says. "And your grocery order won't arrive for two hours."

"I don't need to eat your lunch." He eats healthy foods and I definitely don't want to do that—right now, or ever.

"Well, babe, you need to eat something, otherwise you'll eat *me*, and I don't think either of us want that," he sasses back.

Huffing, I cross my arms over my chest. "I'm not a cannibal."

He rolls his eyes. "Come on, let's go downstairs and get some shawarma. Protein. It'll help."

Grumbling, I get up to follow him. I open the front door and stop.

Because there's Jared, standing on my doorstep.

"What are you doing here?" I demand.

He holds up Yoni's dinosaur print lunchbox. "Yo forgot his lunch."

My knees buckle. Fuck. Why is that so sweet?

"You brought his lunch?"

Jared's cheeks go pink. "He mentioned the *pan esponjado* was your favorite."

It's my turn for my face to go hot. "So you brought *me* lunch."

He swallows. "I plead the fifth."

"We were going to go downstairs for shawarma," I finally say. "Do you want to join us?"

He twitches, his whole body flinching.

But after a moment, he says, "Sure," sounding like it's the last thing he wants to do. Who doesn't like shawarma?

There are footsteps behind me as my assistant makes his way down the hallway.

"Hey, Jare," Yoni says upon seeing his brother. "Oh, you found my lunchbox. Thanks. I was wondering where that went."

"You left it on the kitchen counter," he reports.

"Thanks for bringing it by."

The three of us stand there awkwardly for a beat.

"Okay, I need food before I murder someone for fun," I announce.

Yoni sighs. "Babe, you can't say things like that out loud."

"Why not?"

"Because you don't write murder books. You write sexy books."

I shrug. "A little murder between friends can totally be an aphrodisiac."

Jared mutters something under his breath.

But he doesn't run for the hills at my offbeat sense of humor. Maybe there's promise there after all.

In the shop downstairs, Mo waves us to a table and scurries off to help the rest of the hungry customers in line.

It's a little early for the lunch rush, but today the place is packed. Good. I'm happy for him. Taking over his grandfather's shop wasn't in his plans, especially after he was disowned for marrying a man, so finding out he inherited the shop last year was definitely a surprise.

"What's good here?" Jared asks awkwardly as he lifts a sticky menu.

"You'd like the falafel," Yoni reports. "We get the chicken shawarma."

"No meat shawarma?" Jared teases. Typically, the "beef" shawarma is layered with both beef and lamb.

Yoni's cheeks go pink. "Fuck off," he mutters.

"Yo-yo used to be obsessed with Shari Lewis," he explains.

It takes me a second to place the reference. "Lamb Chop the puppet."

Jared finger-guns at me. It shouldn't be so charming, but I find his awkwardness cute.

"Right. He refused to eat lamb ever since. And considering that's our mother's favorite meal..." He grins at his brother. "I've always appreciated how sensitive he is. He gets a lot of shit for it in the family, but I've never doubted his heart."

Yoni blushes. "Fuck off," he says again. But he's wearing a pleased smile. He likes the praise.

Mo comes by to take our orders. Sure enough, Jared orders the falafel wrap, Yoni gets the chicken shawarma bowl, and I get my usual chicken shawarma fries plate. It's a pile of protein, veggies, pickles, and tabouli over thick-cut fries, all drizzled with zhoug, tzatziki, and hummus to dip.

My stomach grumbles loud enough for both men to hear. Yoni rolls his eyes, and Jared smirks at me.

"Did you take your meds?" My assistant asks.

"Um… I don't remember."

He sighs, shakes his head. "I can't with you." He turns to his brother. "Your numbers are good?"

Jared pulls out his phone, swiping on the screen and then showing it to his brother. "I need to eat something. Good thing we just ordered."

I think back to the continuous glucose monitor on his arm. Aside from the first time we hooked up, ever since it's been virtually unnoticeable. It's just part of him.

"You're diabetic?" I ask casually.

He nods. "Type 2. I was diagnosed about four years ago."

"Huh."

Jared's eyes narrow. "What does that mean?"

"Children," Yoni chides. "Behave."

I shake my head. "Nothing. It seems like you have it handled well."

He shrugs. "I take my meds, I check my numbers, I watch what I eat."

Unbidden, my mind goes to the ravenous way he devoured my pussy—multiple times.

"I'll say," I mutter, my cheeks heating.

He smirks.

Yoni looks between us and shudders. "Do you think Arielle knows of any openings on her team?"

My gaze sharpens on him. "What? You want to jump ship?"

He shakes his head. "No. You know I like working for you." He nods to his brother. "Jare needs a job."

Jared opens his mouth. "Yoni… we talked about this."

"Yeah, well, you're not doing it, so I'm doing it for you," he snaps. He turns to me. "He's been working in sports journalism for a decade. On camera, behind the scenes, statistical analysis, he's done it all. I know Arielle does social media. Does she have any connection to the broadcast team?"

Tapping my mouth with my finger, I think out loud. "They've already started the season, so they're probably full for now. Give it a few months and they might have something."

Yoni winces. "Months?"

"The Grizzlies are wrapping up their season, though…" Hm, now that's a thought. "Van mentioned Jacky is going out on maternity leave soon. It would be short-term, but he'd get his foot in the door."

Jared scoffs. "Can you stop talking about me like I'm not here?"

"Fine. Vanessa works for the Grizzlies in the Logistics department. She could probably get you in on a temp position until something becomes available," I snap. "Do you want me to call her?"

He frowns. "I—"

"Jare, you really can't say no," Yoni tells him gently. "I love you, but you need to put yourself out there. It doesn't need to be forever. It's okay if it's just for now."

Mo interrupts with the tray of food. My stomach reminds me I haven't really eaten the last few days, too engrossed in my book to do much more than make a million cups of coffee and the occasional cheese stick.

"Can you make me some more lunch trays?" I ask Yoni. "They were really helpful."

He smiles gently at me. "Of course, babe. Same as last time?"

"Maybe a different flavor of hummus. The red pepper didn't do it for me. I really like the olive tapenade hummus you get me."

My assistant nods, pulling out his phone and making a note. "I'll swap it out in the grocery order."

Jared looks between us. "He makes you lunch?"

I nod. "Little protein plates with fruits and vegetables in a bento box. Sometimes it's the only thing I eat all day. ADHD means I'm not good at listening to my hunger cues." I stab at a fry covered in chicken and sauce. "Hell, even when I have three alarms and a reminder on my phone, I still forget to take my meds almost every day. And assholes abuse it for fun, which makes it that much harder for me to get it. If he didn't remind me to fill it every month, I'd never have any."

His eyebrows crease. "I'm confused."

Shaking my head, I divert myself. "My meds are a controlled substance. Difficult to remember to fill every month, and when I do remember, half the time the pharmacies are out of stock because people take it recreationally."

"It's totally unfair," Yoni chimes in. "It's not like it's optional. You need the meds. It would be like someone restricting insulin because some people use it to get high."

Jared frowns. "But you don't take it to get high?"

"I use it to *function*. I can't sit in a chair for more than five minutes without fidgeting," I explain. "With meds, I can sit for an entire hour without getting up from my chair and starting something new. Not a whole day. *An hour*. That's all it gets me."

He shakes his head. "Shit. I never thought of it like that."

"It's the same with pain meds. There are legitimate reasons to take narcotic painkillers," I add. "Some people abuse them. It makes it that much harder for people who actually need them to acquire them."

"Only about a quarter of people with Type 2 diabetes take insulin," Jared tells me. "Type 1s are a totally different situation. Despite the pancreas issue, they might as well be two different diseases entirely. But people can't really take insulin recreationally. They won't get high. They'll get dead."

Yoni flinches. "Maybe we can stop talking about murders and deads?"

"Spoilsport," I mutter, and Jared grins at me.

Okay. So maybe he's not *that* bad.

I can do this. I can help him.

But I'm still not doing this for *him*. It's the right thing to do. Yoni needs his brother to get a job. I love Yoni. Thus, I'll help Yoni's brother.

Even if his brother happens to be Jared.

It's as we're heading back upstairs that Jared grabs my arm and pulls me aside.

"I don't need your help," he says harshly.

"I'm not helping *you*," I snap back, wrenching my arm free.

"I can do this on my own."

I scoff.

"I *can*." He blows out a breath. "I don't want this to be misconstrued as asking for something in exchange for sex. We—"

"Don't worry, it's not that," I'm quick to assure him. "I know it doesn't mean anything."

"So you really don't need to—"

"I'm not helping you," I repeat. "I'm helping Yoni's brother."

Jared squints at me. "But *I'm* Yoni's brother."

"Right. But this has nothing to do with *you*, J. It has everything to do with helping my friend."

He blinks a few times. "So this isn't because we hooked up?"

I shake my head. "Get over yourself, babe. You weren't that good."

That's a lie.

And he must be a freaking mind reader, because he smirks. "Is that so?"

"Fuck off," I mutter. "I'll call Vanessa."

Jared sobers. "Sadie, I—"

"But we're not fucking around again," I warn him. That's over and done with. Four times was more than enough.

"Got it," he says, nodding.

Who am I kidding? Four times, and I still haven't gotten my fill.

What the fuck am I supposed to do now?

eighteen

. . .

Jared

JACKY IS A FORMIDABLE WOMAN. She studies me from behind her desk, one hand cupping her swollen belly. She makes me sit in silence for a good few minutes, evaluating me.

I'm not used to being on this side of the scrutiny. Usually, it's me interviewing players and staff, not the other way around.

"Why do you want this job?" she finally asks.

I don't.

But I want *a* job, and this is what's available.

Maybe. Possibly.

I open my mouth, then pause.

"I know this is temporary," I tell her. "I know it doesn't fit with my experience. It gets my foot in the door to hop to a broadcast or media position with the team if one becomes available."

She hums, rubbing her belly. There's movement from within and she flinches.

"Motherfucker—" She hisses.

"Are you feeling okay?" I ask cautiously.

"I'm eight and a half months pregnant with twins," she snarls. "No, I am not feeling okay."

I wince. "That doesn't sound fun."

She blows out a breath. "I'm sorry for snapping. I'm really feeling the discomfort today. And frankly, I don't have any desire to interview some generic dude for a role he's not qualified for, when I have someone already in line for the job, only for him to jump ship at the worst possible time."

She pauses. "But I do appreciate your candor."

"I need a job," I say simply. "I was with the Denver hockey team for four years. Before that, I did a few years with Milwaukee's AHL team and two seasons with Greenville's ECHL team. I've been around the league for a while."

Jacky eyes me. "Why did you leave Denver?"

"My segment had the lowest ratings this past season," I say simply. "Quite frankly, when the team plays as poorly as it did this year, it's difficult to find positive things to say about them. And honestly, I have enough integrity that I'm not going to sugarcoat and pretend the worst team in the league is anything but a disappointment."

She snorts. "I bet management was happy with that."

"They weren't," I say flatly. "I wasn't cruel, I wasn't mean. I was factual. My specialty is statistics and play analysis, and when the play is as poor as they were…" I shrug. "I know hockey. I've been around the sport for a decade. Whether I'm working on the media side or not, I believe I can be of use to your organization, especially with the team pushing for the playoffs."

Jacky narrows her eyes.

"Put me in, coach. Wherever you need help." Steadily, I meet her gaze. "I understand you have someone in position to cover your role. There must be an opening somewhere, something that needs to be backfilled. I'm good with a temp contract. I'm good with something more permanent. I love hockey and want to stay in the league."

She hums, flipping through my resume and references list. "You know Vanessa Morgan?"

"She referred me, yes," I sidestep.

Jacky stares at me.

"We have mutual friends who connected us," I finally explain. "I am very grateful to her for putting my application forward. I don't know her well, but now that I'm living in Boston, I'm looking forward to getting to know her better."

Or at all—since we haven't met in person yet. A few messages exchanged over email is all I've heard from her. Hell, I don't even know what she looks like.

Just that her boyfriend plays for the team and is more of the punch first, ask questions later type.

I totally get it. If anyone else were to look at Sadie crosswise... and she's not even mine.

Fuck.

I really have to stop thinking about her like that. We agreed it was a one-time thing. Each time. It's not like we're intending to sleep together again. Every time it's happened has been a spur-of-the-moment type thing.

She's not interested in more. Neither am I.

Right?

"Hmm."

I can't get a read on whether Jacky's humoring me or actually interested in what I have to say. I wouldn't blame her in the slightest if she's already written me off.

After a few more perfunctory questions, Jacky dismisses me and we go our separate ways. I don't get a tour of the facility; I don't see anything other than the exit.

I'm not in the mood to head home—or rather, to Yoni's place. It doesn't quite feel like home. It's not *mine.* I don't know where I want to live, if I do end up staying in Boston or if I wind up leaving the city. So much is in flux. I don't like it.

The early April chill makes me burrow my hands into my pockets as I walk the streets aimlessly. I haven't explored

Boston. Sure, I've visited before. My brother has lived here for a few years now. Most of my visits to the city were to spend time with him—we hung out at his place, we didn't do the touristy thing.

I want to do the touristy thing.

I lose track of where I am, walking and observing the city. I never did this in Denver, either.

There's a light mist in the air. In an instant, the skies open up and it turns into a downpour. Ducking into the first shop I can see, I am determined to dry off and wait it out.

A chime rings out above me, warning the shoppers of my arrival. Whipping my glasses off my face, I dry them hastily with my soaked jacket before I resettle them and look around.

It's a bookstore.

Cool. I like books.

There's a coffee cart on the left hand side of the store, and as I make my way over there, I pull out my phone to check my numbers. Everything seems pretty stable; a cup of coffee won't hurt.

The person behind the counter is a pretty woman who looks to be in her early twenties. Soft, delicate features, freckles dotting her nose. Her long blonde hair is pulled up into a ponytail, a turquoise streak visible.

She's cute. Pretty. But I don't feel anything for her. I can't remember the last time I felt that fizzle of heat, that draw toward another person.

Well. I can't remember the last time I felt that toward another person *that isn't Sadie.*

Placing my order, I glance around the bookstore as the barista prepares the drink. With no job, I don't really have the discretionary income to go around buying books. And it's not a library—I can't just hang out indefinitely.

My hot coffee in hand, I browse the shelves. I'm a mood reader. It really depends on the day what sort of media I want to immerse myself in. So much of the time, even in my down time, I'm reading press releases and statistical analysis reports; it doesn't always leave time for fun reading.

Now? I have nothing but time on my hands.

The shop is pretty fairly populated. There are at least two or three people browsing per aisle, and the space isn't exactly small. I have to dodge people and winter coats as I meander aimlessly.

There's a big romance section toward the back of the store. Of the books I picked up at that book signing a few weeks ago, I quite enjoyed Leighton's romantic suspense novel. Katja's sapphic fantasy was a breath of fresh air.

Am I turning into a romance reader? Would that really be the worst thing in the world? Surely there's a place for male romance readers in the community.

"What are *you* doing here?"

The female voice cuts through my coffee-and-book haze. My good mood withers like a vine in winter.

Great. Ten seconds in, and I've already ruined this for myself.

An apology on my lips, I turn to the speaker.

But it's not a random Karen.

Sadie.

She's wearing dark jeans and white Keds, a purple smock around her torso. Her wavy hair is pulled back from her face, her makeup neutral and understated. The faint scent of her perfume wafts over me, making my dick react automatically.

"I didn't know you worked here," I tell her mildly, biting back my initial, irrational urge to propose marriage. I don't actually want to get *married*. I just want her.

Sadie scoffs. "Really? He didn't send you here?"

I shake my head. "Went for a walk and needed to escape the rain."

She purses her lips.

"It's good to see you," I offer hopefully. I don't know what

I'm hopeful for. A glimmer of her attention? A scrap of her affection?

"Yeah, whatever," she mutters.

"I met with the Grizzlies today," I add. "Do you mind thanking your friend for me? I really appreciate her referral."

Sadie frowns.

"And yours, of course. You connected us. I can't forget that," I add quickly. "I know you did it to help my brother, but you also helped me at the same time, and I—"

"Shut up," she snaps, her face going red. "I didn't do it for you."

"Can I make it up to you? Buy you coffee?"

Bury my face in her pussy until she screams my name several times over?

"I don't want anything from you," Sadie snaps.

"If I didn't know better, I'd think you didn't like me," I say mildly.

"I don't," she says.

But she can't meet my eyes, her gaze averted toward my shoes.

Stepping closer, I tip her chin up.

"Is that so?" My voice goes down an octave, gritty and dark.

"I don't like you," Sadie says. She swallows loudly.

"The hitch in your breath tells me otherwise." Maybe she isn't as averse to this as she makes it seem.

"It means nothing," she lies. Her pulse flutters wildly in her neck.

"You might not like me," I tell her quietly, "But your body likes what I do to you."

"I don't. It didn't mean anything."

"It doesn't have to mean anything."

Her rich brown eyes dart up to mine, then back down my face. She can't hold my gaze.

Fuck, she is such a good little sub.

"Let me take you out," I urge. "We can have a lot of fun together."

"I don't have time for fun," she argues.

"There's always time for fun."

Sadie opens her mouth to protest.

"Just think about it," I tell her. I press a soft, open-mouth kiss to her lips. "I'm not going anywhere."

nineteen

. . .

Sadie

THE ONLY WAY I function is by utilizing the Do Not Disturb feature on my phone. Still, people know that if they call me enough times, they can bypass this and get to me.

Case in point: my mother.

"I can't talk right now," I tell her as I answer the phone. "Is everything okay?"

"I just miss you," the master manipulator says. "You never call me."

Rolling my eyes, I place my phone on speaker and set it back on my desk. There goes my productivity for the next hour. I move over to my treadmill and start it up. Might as well get some physical activity in during this bitch-fest.

As my mother recounts everything that my sisters and the niblings are up to, I get my steps in. Humming and "yeah"ing every few moments, it's easy to pretend like I actually give a shit.

To be clear: my mom isn't a bad person. She just doesn't get me. She's so preoccupied with appearances and keeping up with the Joneses she fails to recognize that I don't care about any of that.

It wasn't a big deal when I got my nose pierced. Surprisingly, my parents were okay with it. I mean, I was nineteen. Out of the house. On my own. Still, they didn't care.

When I got a ladder of piercings up my ear a year later, they weren't happy, but they recognized it was my body and my decision.

When I broke up with my college boyfriend and moved clear across the country to get away? Yeah, *that* was a big deal. They took it as a personal slight that I needed some distance, and not as me launching into a new phase in my life.

All three of my sisters got married right out of college. Well, Talia got married while in law school, but she was engaged the summer after undergrad. Tamar met her now-husband during her internship her senior year. Sarah and her spouse dated all through college.

And me?

My ex dumped me the day before our college graduation.

I thought I was getting a ring. I didn't particularly *want* one, but I certainly wasn't expecting to be dumped the night our parents met for the "joining of the families" dinner. Dinner, dessert, dumped.

It's been five years and my mother still asks about him. I think I might still follow him on Instagram. Last I knew, Sammy was partying it up in Miami, living his best life. As much as I hold minor resentment for the way it went down, I don't hold ill will toward him. Do I want him to contract a flesh-eating disease and die a gruesome death? Yes. Of course I do. But I don't think about him.

Except when she brings him up.

Which is… every time we talk lately.

The front door opens and shuts.

"Honey, I'm home," Yoni calls out.

"Who's that?" My mother demands.

I roll my eyes.

"Nobody. What did Tamar say?" When in doubt: distract.

Yoni enters my office and, upon catching sight of me on

the treadmill, sighs and shakes his head. He backs slowly out of the room.

A few minutes later, I can hear him puttering around in the kitchen. Good. He knows what to do.

Sure enough, half an hour of being berated later, we say goodbye and I hop off the treadmill. I'm shvitzing like crazy.

In the kitchen, Yoni has set out a charcuterie board of all my favorite junk food. There's cheese and salami, cut fruit and vegetables, and also fun things like sour peach rings, honey mustard pretzels, onion dip and wavy potato chips, and chamoy mango slices. He's uncorked a bottle of rosé, the glass chilled and waiting for me.

"I love you," I declare, falling upon the stool at the kitchen island.

"I'm married," he retorts, and I laugh.

"I didn't say to divorce your spouse," I tease. "I can still love you."

He smiles at me, a little bashful. "Thanks. Right back at you."

Shaking my head, I vow one day to get him to accept a compliment.

"So what did she want?" He asks, digging a chip into the dip.

"What does she ever want?" I roll my eyes. "It was forty-five minutes of talking about nothing."

"Did she bring up Doucheface McGee?"

Tapping my nose, I take a heavy drink from my glass. "How did you guess?"

He sighs. "Have you thought about—"

"Don't you start," I warn.

"I'm just saying, a fake boyfriend would do the trick," Yoni teases.

"Babe, I write romance. I know how that storyline goes."

"I happen to know a guy." He waggles his eyebrows.

"Who do you know that's straight and single?"

He stares at me.

"What?" I drink my wine.

"You know my brother, right?" He scoffs. "Fuck, you guys have hooked up at least—"

"What makes you say that?"

Yoni blinks at me like I'm the dumbest fucking person on the planet. "Babe. I have eyes."

"No, you don't."

"So you didn't sleep with him the night of the Seder?" he asks accusingly.

I shove a chamoy mango in my mouth.

He smirks. "And the convention in Denver…"

Guzzling my wine, I look away.

"Look," he says, his voice softening. "I think he likes you. Your chemistry is clearly off the charts if you've slept with him more than once."

I clear my throat. "We've, um…"

He waits patiently.

"We met on an app. Before Denver," I clarify awkwardly. "It's…"

"Your sub app?"

Yoni pauses. He knows enough about what I like and what I'm looking for. "Wait. That means…"

"I had a good time," I finally say carefully. "But it was only ever meant to be a one-time thing."

Okay, twice.

Three times.

Fuck. I slipped up at the Seder.

Okay. *Four* times. That's it. No more.

Yoni laughs, shakes his head. "Why don't you try something?"

I shrug. "I don't want a relationship."

He blinks at me. "Since when?"

"Since always?"

"You write romance novels," he reminds me. "You love love."

"I do. Love is great," I explain. "Sex with love is awesome. But babe, I can't take care of myself. You are the only reason I'm a halfway functional adult human being. I'm not in a place where I could stand on my own two feet and manage a relationship."

"Or, and hear me out," he says, "You date casually and get laid and be happy?"

I scrunch my face at him.

"It doesn't have to be a serious relationship," Yoni says gently. "There doesn't have to be love and romance. Let him in, just a little bit."

I smirk. "A little?"

He shudders. "Babe, that's my brother."

"Hey, you're the one—"

He throws a slice of bell pepper at me. "I meant into your heart. Let him into your pussy as much as you want, even if that's not at all. He's a good guy."

"You have to say that. He's your brother."

"Yeah, he's my brother," Yoni repeats slowly. "I think you should date my brother."

I chew my lip.

"I mean, he's not a doctor or a lawyer or anything, but he's pretty cute, if I do say so myself." He winks. "Go out a few times, get laid. If you get along well enough, bring him to your parents' anniversary party in a few months."

I bolt upright.

The anniversary party.

"You don't seriously think…"

Yoni shrugs. "If nothing else, he can be a good buffer."

"Yeah, and then my mother will ask about him for the next five years," I gripe.

"She might," he allows. "Or it could turn into happily ever after and—"

This time, I throw an apple slice at him. He catches it in his mouth.

"Shut up," I mutter.

Happily ever after is a lot of pressure to put on a hookup.

And that's all it's been. A hookup. I haven't spent any time with Jared—on purpose. My body sings out when his is near, craving his attention.

I have to face it: he's part of my social circle now. We're going to keep running into each other.

Should I just go out on a freaking date with him?

The sex is good. Fuck, the sex is phenomenal. Do I want more than that? What if he turns me down?

No. He came to the bookstore. He asked me to coffee. I'll buy that he didn't seek me out, but once we crashed into each other…

"Okay, fine," I finally say.

Yoni's face lights up. "You'll go out with him?"

Against my better judgment, I nod. "Are you going to tell him? Or should I?"

He laughs. "I think it will be better coming from you."

twenty

· · ·

Jared

THE CRAFT FAIR is my idea of hell. It's misting rain outside, a bite to the air warning of more to come, and I'm supposed to stand guard over Sadie's table while she meets readers.

I shouldn't even be here. I hadn't planned on coming to the street fair. But when Yoni crawled into my room at four o'clock in the morning and told me he was dying of the plague, I knew I'd take his place today. Elliott is at home, playing nursemaid, so I'm playing bodyguard.

Not that she's acknowledged me since I showed up to her place early this morning. We packed up the ride-share with her boxes of books, drove out to Newton, and set up entirely in silence. She pointed where things went. At one point, she disappeared entirely.

But then she came back holding two coffee cups, silently offering one to me. So maybe she's thawing. Hopefully.

There have been a steady stream of looky-loos, but not many sales so far. Sadie has her bright and charming Sylvie smile on.

A large man stops beside her table, his head cocked as he takes in the books displayed. With a quiet grunt, he nods and picks up a title. He's at least six foot six and has the broad frame of someone who works out. Clutched in his fist is a hefty tote bag packed full with books.

Sadie falls silent. She has a way of reading the reader, knowing when they want a sales pitch and when they need to be coaxed out of their shell.

The man looks at his smartwatch, then sighs. He pulls his phone out of his pocket and types something in a message.

Almost immediately, his phone rings.

"Yes, babe, I know," he says without waiting for the other person to respond.

"Sylvie Hirsch!" A woman's voice shrieks on the other end. "Are you fucking kidding me?"

The man sighs. "So you want them all, then?"

"You bet your ass I do," the woman says loudly through the line. "Does she have the special edition?"

Sadie nods, lifting the title.

"Here, hang on a second," the man says. "Do you mind?" He asks Sadie.

She shakes her head.

"Okay, babe, you're on speaker," he says.

The woman lets out a high-pitched shriek. "OMG! Sylvie Hirsch!"

Sadie grins from ear to ear. "Hi, there. Who am I talking to?"

"My name is Mackenzie and I am *such* a fan!" The woman says. "I'm out of town this weekend but when I heard you were coming by, I told Wes he *had* to come see you."

"I'm glad he did," she says. Her eyes flicker to mine, her smile softening.

"I work for a small independent bookstore in Newton," Mackenzie continues. "We carry all of your books."

"I'll get the name of the bookstore from—Wes, you said?"

The man nods.

"And we'll figure out a way for me to stop by and sign some of your stock," Sadie offers.

Mackenzie lets out a shriek. "You'd do that?"

"Absolutely. I'll get the information and reach out to you," she promises.

Wes beams.

She clicks off the call. "Thank you. That was amazing," she says.

He shakes his head. "You're the amazing one. She absolutely loves your books." He clears his throat. "I do, too."

"Romance is for everyone," I chime in.

Sadie swivels her head to stare at me.

"Oh?" I ask lightly. "Do you not agree?"

She closes her eyes and presses her lips together. "I can't deal with you right now." She turns back to Wes. "Let me get the details."

Ten minutes later, he leaves with another enormous tote bag of books. He bought one of nearly each title, plus the two different special edition box sets.

"What are you doing here?" Sadie demands after he leaves.

"I told you. Yoni has the stomach flu."

"Yeah. But what are you doing *here*?"

I bite the inside of my cheek. "Is it so strange to believe I want to spend time with you?"

"Yes," she says immediately. "You don't want to do that."

"Why not?"

"You just want to fuck me and move on," she counters.

"Or, and hear me out," I say lightly. "I can want to fuck you and also want to spend time with you."

She blinks a few times. "Really?"

I shrug. "We're good together."

"Yeah, but..." She looks away, crossing her arms over her chest. "This isn't the time."

"It's not," I agree. "Can I take you to dinner?"

She opens her mouth, closes it. "Um…"

"Seriously, just a meal," I add. "No expectations. We'll have a nice evening together. That's all it has to be."

Sadie chews her cheek. "Okay," she finally says.

My heart soars inside my chest, roaring with pleasure.

"Okay," I agree, unable to hide my pleased smile.

She rolls her eyes. "Shut up," she mutters, fidgeting with the tablecloth in front of her.

I nudge my shoulder against hers, relishing the contact when she doesn't squirm away.

"Okay," I repeat softly.

———

By the time the street fair is over, everything packed up, and then shlepped across town to Sadie's place, I'm wiped. I have no idea how she manages this on the regular.

"I want to take you out," I confess as I drop onto her couch. "I don't think I can do it tonight, though."

"Oh? Chickening out?" A smirk curves her lips.

"Brat." I shake my head. "I ought to put you across my lap and spank you for that."

She inhales sharply.

"I don't think I have the energy, though," I admit.

"Do you want me to order something in?" She asks nervously. "You don't have to go home right away."

My chest bursts with hope. "That would be great."

She putters around the house for a few minutes before she collapses on the sofa across from mine. Draping an arm over her forehead, she busies herself on her phone.

Her eyes are tired, her face weary, but there's a lightness to her spirit that exudes from her pores. She's content.

So am I.

Even though I keep feeling her eyes on me, whenever I look up, her gaze is averted. My dick reacts automatically to her submission. We don't have to be in a scene for me to want her; it's a default setting, I want her all the time.

We haven't spent much time with our clothes on. From the little we have, though, I know I want to get to know her more. She intrigues me. I want to know everything.

Half an hour later, the doorbell rings, and Sadie forces herself upright. She putters down the hallway toward the door, coming back a few moments later with two big brown bags of food.

"I didn't know what you wanted, so I got a little of every-thing," she says.

I blink. "So you got… everything?"

She nods. "I figure what we don't eat tonight, I'll have as leftovers this week."

"Fuck, I love you," I blurt.

Her eyes go wide.

I clap my hand over my mouth. "I didn't mean it that way."

"Good, because I barely know you," she says, but a smile curves her lips.

"I'm going to wash up." I don't know why I feel the need to announce this.

She laughs, shaking her head.

On my way past her, I swat her lightly on the hip, and her eyes go bright.

"We're not in a scene," she teases.

"We could be," I counter. Dropping a light kiss on her cheek, I squeeze her shoulder. "But I do want to get to know you. No sex, just this."

"That sounds nice." Her voice is soft, wistful. "I don't know the last time I did that."

"Get used to it, babe." I wink as I edge past her toward the half bath.

Taking care of business, I wash my hands and run a hand through my messy curls. It's almost time to get my hair cut again. My beard could use a trim, too. I didn't have a chance this morning with the unexpected change in plans. My shirt is wrinkled and a little sweaty, a streak of dirt on the flank.

All in all: not the look I wanted for our first date.

Is this our first date? Or is this a precursor to our date?

In the main room, Sadie has set out a veritable feast of what smells like Chinese food. A dozen black plastic containers containing rice, noodles, soup, and every dish I can think of wait for us.

Sadie hands me a bowl and a set of chopsticks along with a fork.

"How do you feel about shrimp in lobster sauce?" she asks seriously.

I laugh. "I don't keep kosher."

"Cool. Me, neither." She's nonchalant about it. "It's always kind of awkward bringing it up. Like, my family didn't do it growing up, but whenever I'm with someone else that's Jewish, I always wonder if they're judging me if I'm Jewish *enough*."

"I'm not judging you or anyone else." I help myself to some sweet and sour pork, taking care to pick out some pineapple chunks. My favorite. "I know what you mean, though. I'm not religious. I don't know the last time I went to temple, actually. But I'm still Jewish and I still identify with the culture. It's such a big part of me."

Sadie blinks a few times. "Yes. That's it exactly."

"It's an ethnicity as well as a religion. People who aren't part of it don't get it."

"They don't," she says quietly. "I'm working hard to cultivate friendships with other Jewish people as an adult, not just the kids I knew from camp growing up. Same as I try to cultivate friendships with other neurodivergent people and other romance writers. I want to surround myself with people like me."

My stomach tumbles. "That sounds really nice. You can carve out a community for yourself."

Her cheeks go pink. "So, um, how are you settling in? You like the job?"

"I'm enjoying it so far." I didn't get the Logistics Director temp job—that went to Vanessa—but someone else moved into her role, and I was brought on to cover theirs. "It's similar to what I did before, yet still different enough to be a challenge."

She shakes her head. "I don't get it."

"Get what?" I twirl some of the lo mein noodles around my chopsticks and succeed only in dropping them all over my shirt.

Smiling, Sadie passes me a napkin. "I mean, seeing you in real life… it's hard to connect the nice guy with the Dom," she says.

"I'm not that nice," I tell her honestly.

She scoffs.

"I care more about bringing my partner pleasure than mine. It typically means putting my needs aside for theirs." I shrug. "I don't need to be in control. I just like it."

She chews on her lip. "Your profile… it says you don't want a relationship."

"When I was traveling three-quarters of the year, I didn't have the energy for a long-distance relationship," I clarify. "I'm no longer traveling for work. I don't know that I'll get back in the broadcast studio anytime soon. More than that," I stress, "I didn't want to disappoint someone by being emotionally unavailable on top of being physically unavailable. That was too much."

"You consider yourself emotionally unavailable?"

I shrug again. "Casual sex was always easier."

"Oh." She looks down.

"But—"

Sadie's eyes dart to mine, then back to the floor.

"I'm in Boston for the long term," I tell her. "I've decided I want to stay here. Unless I magically get my dream job somewhere else, I'm staying in town."

"What's your dream job?"

I chew my lip. "Promise you won't laugh?"

She inhales sharply. "Promise."

"I want to do studio analytics for the NHL," I admit. "I don't have a degree in statistics, my background is in journalism, but half those dudes don't have the qualifications, either."

"And that would be… where?"

"Jersey."

"Oh." She looks away.

"But this is a long-shot pipe dream," I am quick to add. "And I—well, I don't know that I'd ever get the opportunity to do it. If I had to pie-in-the-sky dream, though… that would be it. *And* it wouldn't involve a lot of travel. It would be in-studio."

twenty-one

• • •

Sadie

I DON'T KNOW how I feel about this.

Jared's only here temporarily. I can feel it in my bones. This is just a stopover until he gets to where he wants to be.

Why can't it be easy and casual? Why does it have to be all or nothing? I can hear Yoni's voice in the back of my head. It's a little disconcerting that the brother of the man I want to fuck is the one in my head, but hey, weirder things have happened, I guess.

"I don't know how to do this," I admit out loud.

"Do what?" Jared squints at me from behind his black plastic glasses frames.

"You want to date," I tell him.

He nods.

"You want to date *me.*"

"Is that so hard to believe?"

"I don't… do that."

"You don't date?" He sounds skeptical.

I lift a shoulder. "Sex only. No feelings. It's easier that way."

"Are you concerned you won't have feelings for me?"

I open my mouth.

"Or are you concerned that you *will*?" His eyes are bright as they focus on mine.

I want to wipe that stupid smirk off his lips. With my mouth.

"Fuck, we're really getting into it," I mutter, reaching for an egg roll.

"Am I making you uncomfortable?" He asks.

I shake my head. "Not you. The subject matter… I don't like talking about it in general."

"Ah."

"It has nothing to do with you. It would be the same with anyone else."

To my surprise, he gives me a smile. Dryly, he says, "I'm glad."

I crack a smile, too. "I like being independent. I'm on my own a lot, or I'm writing and off in my head, or I'm traveling for book signings and retreats. And that doesn't include my full-time job. Most men are not okay if they aren't my number one priority."

"I'm not most men," Jared says mildly.

"So you wouldn't feel neglected if—"

"No," he interrupts.

"But—"

"No," he says firmly. "As long as you communicate about your availability, both emotional and physical, I won't be scared away by you living your life."

I swallow.

"There aren't a lot of things I require in a relationship," he continues. "Monogamy is the big one. Communication, too. The rest of it? Fuck, I travel for work a lot, too. I could hardly blame you for not wanting to start something with me. I'd be more upset if you were giving up your life and your hobbies to make room for me."

"You'd be surprised," I mutter.

Jared scoots toward me, putting his finger under my chin

and tipping it up.

"I'm not him," he says firmly. "Whoever he was, whoever hurt you. *I am not him*. I won't do that to you."

My skin prickles with unease. I try to lower my gaze. His firm grip on my chin keeps my eyes on his.

"I like you exactly as you are," Jared says. "You're fun and vibrant and creative. You have *ideas*. You have this natural magnetism that draws in the people around you. I want to know you. I want to know more."

"I can barely take care of myself half the time," I admit. "Your brother has to make sure I eat regularly and drink enough water."

Jared rolls his eyes. "He calls me his houseplant. Because he constantly checks my numbers and if I'm doing okay."

I gape at him. "I thought it was just me he doted on."

"He does it for the people he loves," he says. "And he loves you."

Balling up my napkin, I toss it onto the table. "So what does it mean for us that he has to take care of us?"

"It means we have someone who cares for us," Jared shrugs. "And hell, maybe that's the missing piece we need in a relationship. Someone outside to take care of things like watering the plants and walking the dog."

"You want your brother to be the third in our relationship?" I tease.

He chokes. "In a non-sexual way? Yeah."

My eyes go round.

"He already runs both of our lives. It would probably be easier for him," he adds. "Saves him the headache."

"I can't believe we're talking about a relationship." I shake my head. "I just agreed to one date."

Jared grins at me. "It's important to establish parameters. You have to consent just like if it were a scene."

"Okay? So what are your limits?"

He pauses. "I don't think I want to get married."

"At all?"

"I'm interested in a long-term committed partnership," he says. "The formality of marriage isn't important to me. But if my partner insisted, I would." He takes a breath. "I was engaged before. It ended for a variety of reasons. But I don't know that I'd want to go through with that again."

"I don't know that I'd want to subject a partner to my family," I admit quietly. "They're... well, there's a reason I don't spend a lot of time with them."

"That's the wrong way to look at it," Jared says. "In a healthy partnership, the family is the people who are in the relationship. Whether it's a couple or a polycule, the center of gravity shifts. You are a self-sufficient adult. The family of origin doesn't go away, don't get me wrong. But the partner should stand beside you and support you, allow you the strength to navigate those relationships on your terms."

Huffing a laugh, I mutter, "that's cute," before I violently break apart a fortune cookie.

Jared's eyes pin me to my chair. "If that didn't happen in the past, they weren't the right partner."

I bite my lip. "But you are?"

He lifts a shoulder. "I'm willing to try."

Opening my mouth, he cuts me off.

"I'm not saying I'm perfect or that everything will be smooth sailing. I'm human. I make mistakes. And honestly, I haven't tried for a relationship in years." He pauses, his eyes glued to mine. "But you're the one I want to try this with."

Plucking at a loose thread in my sweater, I ask quietly: "Why me?"

His brown eyes are a rich amber, light and bright. "It was only ever supposed to be a one-time thing. That's what we agreed to, right?"

I nod.

"So why have we hooked up four times in three cities? What keeps bringing us together?"

"An app?" I guess.

Jared shakes his head. "I'd like to think it's fate."

Oh.

"We don't have to get married and have a million babies. We can just date for a while and see if we're compatible," he says.

I chew my lip again.

"What is it?" He leans forward, tugging my lip free.

"I don't want kids," I admit.

He blinks.

"Is that a dealbreaker?"

Jared exhales slowly. "Not at all. I'm not crazy about the idea, either."

"I did…" Blowing out a breath, I squeeze my eyes shut for courage, then open them again. "I offered Yoni and El my eggs. I told them I'd be a surrogate if they want."

He blinks a few times. "You would do that?"

Slowly, I nod. "It's not like I need them. And they would be great parents."

Jared rushes forward, toppling his chair, and scoops me into a hug. His arms are tight around me, his scent enveloping me in the most perfect cocoon.

"You're the best person I've ever met," he declares.

"Oh, I don't know…"

"You are." He squeezes me tighter. "I can't believe you'd do that for my brother. I—*Thank you.*"

"They haven't taken me up on it yet," I mutter. "They're still thinking it over."

"Still. That you would even offer…"

He releases me, but he doesn't go far. His thumb trails my cheek, his eyes bright.

"You really care for him, don't you?"

I nod. "He's my other half. I don't function without him."

Jared chuckles. "I'm glad it's my brother and not some random man."

My eyebrows go up.

"I can trust my brother will take care of you and love you and nurture you. He won't take your shit and he won't coddle you. And he won't take advantage of you."

"So you don't mind that another man is my other half?" I can't imagine that he would possibly be okay with this….

He shakes his head. "I have no right to influence who you bring into your life. We're just starting this journey together. But—and this is the big thing—I have to trust you, and you have to trust me. And I'm glad you have someone in your corner that I already know and trust will take care of you the way I would."

"Well, I'm not going to sleep with him," I tease.

"Good. Because I don't share." Jared smacks a kiss to my lips, pulling away before I can respond. "Ethical non-monogamy isn't for me. I'm okay with sharing in the context of a scene, where we both consent with specific limits and parameters, but I'm not interested in a polycule or opening up the relationship."

"Me, either." I don't even know how I feel about the relationship as a whole. I'm not ready to add anyone else to the mix on top of it.

Jared strokes his thumb along my cheek again, his dark brown eyes bright with happiness.

"I'm glad we're doing this," he says. "Thank you for giving me a chance."

"Me, too," I say.

And to my surprise, it's true.

His hand curls around to my neck, gripping lightly. A warm buzz runs through my veins, warming me from the inside out. I love me a good hand necklace.

When he lowers his lips to mine, it's with the firm knowledge that we're on the same page. The kiss isn't about lust. He's not trying to get me naked.

He tastes me, explores me. His lips are soft, coaxing mine

apart. Unbidden, I gasp, and he surges forward, deepening the kiss.

My hands fist in his shirt, holding him close. We're already chest to chest, belly to belly, but I need him closer, closer, inside my veins like a drug.

Jared pulls back, but he doesn't go far. "I should go."

"You don't have to." My words come out breathy, and he gives me a warm smile.

"I should. It's late and you have an early morning at the bookstore tomorrow."

Exaggerating my pout, I tease, "I don't even get a *yay, we're dating* fuck?"

He laughs. "That's what we have to look forward to."

twenty-two

. . .

Sadie

CECI WANTED to go to a hockey game, so I'm at a hockey game. Vanessa is down at ice level, working, and I know Jared is around the building somewhere. He offered to get me a comp ticket, but Ceci being Ceci, that wasn't necessary.

It's nice to have some time with my friends. Johanna is chill and Sullivan is my bud. Rory works with his brother-in-law Josh and is slowly being brought into our circle. Bex and Elsy both have hockey ties and know the ins and outs of all the player drama. Hazel and Leah are a barrel of laughs, recounting all the hockey romances they've read and comparing the players to their book boyfriends.

I wish *my* boyfriend was here. In the three weeks since we've been together, we've gone on a handful of dates. It's like once that initial band-aid was ripped off, so was Jared's composure. We've slept together after each date since—except for one night that his sugar was a little high, and he needed to monitor it a little more closely.

Sometimes we go out. Sometimes we stay in. One thing's a definite: we have a good time together.

This whole relationship thing is *easy*. Not the relationship interpersonal stuff, but the simple act of *being* in the relationship. I like having someone I can talk to about my thoughts and feelings, someone who cares about my wants and needs. It's different with my friends and with Yoni.

With Jared… it means more. I can't really describe *why*, just that it does.

And yes, I like having someone I can call for sex on demand. That part's pretty great, too.

I miss you, Jared's texted.

My heart melts. I'm sure I have a schmoopy look on my face because Sullivan laughs and snaps a photo.

"You're ridiculous," he taunts.

"Go to hell," I toss back, smiling at my phone screen.

Someone shuffles through the row ahead of us. Even though it's intermission, it's still annoying. I open my mouth to bitch at them and stop.

Because Jared is standing in front of me, a cup of beer in one hand and a bucket of popcorn in the other.

"Thought you might need some snacks," he says.

"What are you doing here?" I demand.

Sullivan reaches forward and takes the beer, passing Johanna the popcorn bucket. Jerk. That's mine.

But I can't say anything, because my brain is going haywire at the sight of my boyfriend.

"Don't you have to work?"

"I'm taking a quick break," Jared says, his eyes bright. "Did you get my text?"

My heart is in my throat as I nod dumbly.

"I missed you, too," I say quietly.

"Good thing I knew where to find you." He winks outlandishly and I laugh.

"Kiss! Kiss! Kiss!" chants the crowd.

I look up to find the Kiss Cam trained straight on us.

"So, how 'bout it?" Jared teases.

Yanking him forward by his team polo, I bring him to my level and kiss the ever-loving shit out of him. My arms wind around his neck and he reaches for me, half-lifting me out of my seat and supporting my weight as he kisses me back.

My whole world explodes and then narrows in on this moment, this infinite bliss. Jared is like a breath of fresh air. He makes me believe that love really is possible, that it's an actual possibility for me.

I've always been headstrong. When I was little, they thought it might have been Oppositional Defiant Disorder, but as I grew up and learned to regulate, my fight or flight instinct tampered down.

I've still got a stubborn streak a mile wide, though.

With Jared, though, I don't feel like that's a bad thing. He *likes* that I'm independent, that I can take care of myself—mostly—and don't need to be waited on hand and foot all the time. Do I like to be pampered? Yes, of course. Do I need it all the time? No. It would drive me mad.

And as much as he likes to take care of me and bring me pleasure in the bedroom, he doesn't want someone subservient outside of it. He wants an equal—and so do I.

He makes me feel like my wants and needs are just as important as his. I've never had that before. I'm so used to being shoved aside, being the least important person in the equation. With my parents, with my siblings, even with some of my friends.

It's why I cut ties with so many people from Scottsdale. It's why I don't keep in touch with the people I knew in college.

This is the new me: take it or leave it.

Jared cups my cheek, the simple contact bringing me back to the moment.

"Will you come home with me?" he asks quietly.

I tilt my head. "To Yoni's?"

He smiles. "Okay. Can I go home with you?"

Sullivan clears his throat.

We both turn to look at him.

"Go away," I tell my bestie.

He rolls his eyes. "Dude. Invite him to the bar."

I turn back to Jared. "We're going to a bar after the game. You should come with me."

He opens his mouth.

"And then *after*, we'll go home together," I add.

He grins. "That sounds great."

Sullivan smirks at us, and I reach over and punch him in the shoulder.

"I'll introduce you to everyone properly then," I promise.

Jared kisses my nose. "Looking forward to it."

He releases me to my seat and edges back along the row ahead of us. His broad form cuts an impressive picture, his dark jeans clinging tightly to his thick ass and thighs.

"Damn," Ceci says. "That is one serious hunk of a man."

"I know." I grin. "And he's mine."

"Get it, girl," Bex says, lifting her hand for a high-five across the three people between us. "Does he have a brother?"

I laugh. "Yeah, he's married."

"Damn." She shakes her head. "You get all the fucks. I mean, the luck."

"Yeah, that too." I grin at her.

"He's good to you?" Rory asks quietly, a frown between her eyebrows.

Nodding, I think back over the last few weeks. "It's new, but it's been pretty great so far."

"I'm happy for you, babe," Sullivan says, squeezing my shoulder. "You've been waiting for this for a long time."

"What? No, I haven't. I don't date." I shake my head. "I didn't date. But that was on purpose."

"Yeah. And now you found someone that made you change your mind about that." He nudges me. "That's not a bad thing. When you wanted to be single, you were single. When you found the right guy, you did something about it."

"I don't know that he's the right guy…"

Elsy raises her eyebrows. "What's wrong with him?"

"Nothing. It's just—we've only been together for a little while. We're still getting to know each other."

She sighs. "Just don't wish away a good thing looking for the bad. He might genuinely be a good person."

Elsy's coming off a rough breakup with the second chair clarinetist in her symphony. She's been pretty tight-lipped about what happened, only that it was *not* a mutual decision and decidedly *not* amicable. Even her music isn't bringing her solace these days.

My heart aches for her pain. She is such a good egg. All she wants is to love and be loved in return.

Sometimes I wonder if I'm missing that gene. Since Sammy imploded my life five years ago, relationships were the last thing I wanted. I didn't *want* to be with anyone. I went out, I hooked up, and got my needs met.

But with Jared... I like coming together at the end of the day. Whether I've been in the writing cave or at the bookstore, he always asks about my day and what I've been working on. He's offered suggestions when I've been stuck on a plot point and rubbed my feet while I vented about the new hire at the shop. He *cares*.

I'm not used to someone caring about me.

Oh, I'm sure my friends do. They love me, and I love them. But it's a different kind of caring, surface-level and cursory.

Sullivan passes me the popcorn. Johanna's barely made a dent in it, which is fine, because there's enough for all nine of us to partake and still have leftovers.

"How's the book coming along?" he asks lightly.

"I'm in the part where they're falling in love but too dumb to notice it," I report.

He hums.

"What?"

"Sound familiar?" he teases.

I scrunch my face. "No?"

With a snort, he shakes his head. "You're cute."

Johanna, on his other side, looks over at us. "She is cute," she comments blandly. "I still don't do threesomes."

I choke.

"You know I only have eyes for you, babe," Sullivan says, wrapping his arm around her shoulder.

She laughs, leaning into his embrace, but when I catch her eye, she winks.

She knows I'm not trying to encroach on her man. She's got him wrapped around her pinky finger just fine on her own.

As the third period starts up and play resumes on the ice, I lose myself in the comfortable familiarity of the game. Between Ceci and Vanessa's connections to the team and my own research for my books, I've spent *a lot* of time watching hockey. I've been in Boston for five years and am a genuine fan of the black and gold Grizzlies.

Who would have thought a sports-averse girl from Arizona would become a sports romance writer who *actually* enjoys watching sports? I used to call all athletic endeavors "sportsball" because it was so boring to me. And now I genuinely enjoy watching and even, gasp, participating.

Sometimes. Watching is usually more fun. Especially with all the eye-candy.

Ceci leans over and points out a player. "See McKittrick? He's on a points streak. Five games."

I nod. He's a veteran on the team. Earlier this season, he spent more time in the press box than on the ice. I'm not sure what's changed over the last few months, but now that they're in the playoff push, he's playing every game.

"I heard he's thinking of retiring," Ceci whispers.

My eyebrows go up. "But he has two more years left on his contract!"

She shrugs. "Just a rumor. Don't tell anyone."

I laugh. "You just told me."

"Thought you could use it for a storyline. Aging team captain turns it around in his final season to hoist the Cup." Ceci winks at me. "I mean, we can hope, right?"

"That would be nice," I agree.

What would make it even more sweet?

Sharing that experience with someone.

Like… maybe Jared?

My breath catches. I've never *wanted* to share milestones like that with anyone. My family never cared; my friends have enough going on.

But with Jared… I can see myself relying on him, trusting him. I'm not there yet. It's still early days for us.

One day—soon.

twenty-three

· · ·

Jared

THE BAR IS loud and packed, the crowd raucous after an exciting playoff win. I can hardly blame their enthusiasm. Even hiding away at my desk, watching on my monitor as I filed paperwork, the atmosphere was electric.

Sadie texted me that she was in the VIP section of the bar. I flash my employee badge at the bouncer and he lets me through.

I recognize some of her friends from earlier. Vanessa, my new coworker, is cuddled up with Sven Larsson, her hockey player boyfriend. He brought a few of his teammates along for the social hour, though he seems content to drink his beer and ignore everyone else.

I've only met him once—in the cafeteria, where I was getting coffee for the entire logistics department—but he seemed nice enough, if a little standoffish. Vanessa mentioned he's been working on unmasking as much as possible. I commend him for that. I can't imagine how difficult it must be to unlearn all of the social niceties and simply be comfortable in his own skin.

Sadie beams at me from across the table as I make my way

over to her. That guy is next to her again, his arm around a pretty Asian woman, her nose in her e-reader.

My girlfriend pulls me into the empty chair and I immediately wrap my arm around her, breathing in her fresh, fruity perfume and the honeydew-scented hair products she uses.

In just a few short weeks, she's managed to get under my skin in the best way possible. We're keeping it casual—a few evenings together a week, plenty of distance for us both to live our lives—but there's something about the familiar certainty that at the end of the night, we'll be going home together.

I don't have any friends in the city yet. Usually the way I get to know people is through the kink scene. Hmm… I wonder if Sadie would be interested in checking out a sex club with me…

Shaking my head, I focus on the moment. Tonight is for me to meet her friends.

A gorgeous olive-skinned woman wearing a leather jacket, a blood-red corset beneath it, plops into the seat across from me. Her hair falls in spiral coils halfway down her back, a shimmery wave of chestnut and auburn curls.

"Hi, I'm Cecilia, but you can call me Ceci," she says, offering her hand for a shake. "We're so glad you're here with us."

"Thanks. Happy to meet you."

And it's true. Sadie's warned me Ceci is the social ringleader. Once I get on her good side, I'll be in with the rest of the group.

But as much as I want to make a good impression, I want to get along with her friends for Sadie's sake. I don't ever want to put her in a position where she has to choose between me or her friends.

Ceci sets her hand on my forearm, squeezing gently. "Do you want a drink?"

"Oh, I'm okay for now. Thanks, though." I meet her eyes with a steady smile.

"I could use another," the other man at the table says. "Babe, you want anything?"

But he's not looking to his girlfriend, the woman he's wrapped around. He's looking at Sadie.

"Just a water. Thanks, boo," my girlfriend says.

Very curious about this dynamic, I look back and forth between them a bit.

"Hey, man," he says, holding out his hand. "I'm Sullivan."

He's a broad, beefy dude with a soft belly and a scruffy beard. His Boston Grizzlies t-shirt is a little tight in the chest and shoulders, like he's put on weight since the last time he wore it.

I feel that. Half the time, my clothes are tighter than I remember them being.

"Jared." To my surprise, he doesn't try to squeeze me out; he just shakes my hand.

I look to the dark-haired woman beside him.

"Johanna," she says, looking up from her e-reader, forcing a smile, and then delving back into her book. "I don't like loud places."

It's only then that I recognize she's wearing in-ear headphones.

Sullivan squeezes Sadie's shoulder. "Be right back."

Scooting my chair closer, I murmur quietly in her ear. "What's the deal with that guy?"

"What do you mean?" She tucks a curl behind her ear and it immediately springs forward again. I smooth it back and she leans her head into my palm.

"He called you babe."

"Oh. That's just Sully." She shrugs. "He's my bestie."

She's mentioned him only in the context of the larger group. I didn't know they were *that* close.

"You know how I feel about sharing…"

Sadie laughs loudly. "Don't worry, our interests are *not* compatible," she says. "Also, Johanna doesn't share, either."

I'm a little confused why she's at the bar if she's sensitive to noise and doesn't want to socialize.

"Jo likes hockey, and so does Sully for that matter, but he's here to hang out with the rest of the group. They compromise," Sadie explains. "She prefers more intimate settings like the book club nights at the store. He likes the loud and raucous, always loves a good party."

"So this way they have a little of both," I realize slowly.

She nods. "It's important to know your limits. She warns us when she's getting overstimulated and needs to bounce. He's good at supporting her and leaving her be when she needs space."

"And you two have never…?" I raise my eyebrows.

Sadie makes a face. "Ew. No. He's my drinking buddy. We go out and have a good time. In fact, he's the one who told me about our app. His brother used to use it."

"Oh? What changed?"

"He found his now husband," she says simply.

"Ah. That would do it."

I feel awkward and uncomfortable in my skin. We've talked about marriage, we've established that neither of us are interested in that, but while I'm not opposed to a long-term committed partnership, I know she's still skittish. I don't know how to get her to see that there are more options available for us to build a life together than a ring and a white dress that neither of us want.

In the circles both of us were raised in, there were strict parameters for how our lives were supposed to go. College, then marriage, then babies, and in that order. Any deviation from that invited public commentary on something that should have truly been a private matter.

She's mentioned a few times that she's happier with the

distance from her family. She can love them and still want some space. I certainly don't want my parents on top of me.

With Yoni, it's different. He treats me like an equal. Even though I still want to take care of my younger brother, I'm trying hard to see him as a grown adult capable of making his own life decisions. I don't want to infantilize him like my parents have done for so long.

Sadie gets a double dose of that from her family, being both the youngest child and the only one who deviated from the expected path. What her family can't see—what she can't show them, and what they aren't receptive to acknowledging —is that she is perfectly happy with her life just the way it is. She doesn't need a husband or babies to fulfill her. She doesn't need a traditional 9-to-5 job to bring her joy. Despite what her parents think, there's no shame in managing a bookstore.

Sullivan returns with a tray of drinks. He hands Sadie a water bottle and Johanna a shot of tequila, then passes Ceci a beer and two more down to the other end of the table.

Sadie squeezes my arm. "Let's meet the rest of the gang."

Bex is a busty redhead wearing a Philadelphia Whitney jersey. That's right; the brawler is her brother. She's working on her Ph.D. in ethical biostatistics, Sadie tells me proudly.

Beside her is Elsy, a plus-size blonde who sits first chair violin for the Boston Symphony. Rory, Hazel, and Leah are more engrossed in the trio of hockey players at the next table.

Vanessa and Sven sit between them, bridging the gap between the two groups. She gives me a smile and goes back to her conversation with Elsy and Bex.

Larsson gives me an up-nod. He seems like a decent dude. His beer is mostly full, despite having been here for over an hour, and his face belies his exhaustion. He played a heavy-hitting game. Although the team lost in overtime, it was a high-scoring, high-excitement game all the way through.

This is the kind of game I would have loved to pick apart

and analyze. At two different points, the Grizzlies were up over the Storm, but at the end of the night, they couldn't close the deal.

I like this job, working in the Logistics department. It's fine. It's a job.

But if the last month has taught me anything, it's that I don't want to do this full-time forever. I want to do the deep diving statistical analysis that makes me happy.

Now I just have to figure out how.

twenty-four

. . .

Sadie

"OKAY, GIRL. SPILL."

Rachel winces. "There's nothing to spill. It's fine."

I fix her with a glare. "Sweetheart. Monkey. Angel. Talk to me."

"Okaaaaaay." She takes a sip of her mimosa. "He's fine. He's just....We're not moving forward."

I raise my eyebrows.

She's been vague about what's up with her and Erik, but the last two times I saw her, she didn't look happy. At the Seder six weeks ago, she was downright miserable. I cashed in on our promised brunch and waited for drinks to be served before ensnaring her in my trap.

My heart hurts for my friend. She's so gentle, so kind. She gives so much. All I want is for her to be loved by someone who deserves her.

"He made all these promises about getting married, and I don't want to give him an ultimatum, but he said three years ago he wanted to propose. And I don't want him to *propose*, per se. An engagement means nothing if there isn't a wedding date and then a future planned after it. I don't need a ring—I want us to be married. I want us to embark on the next stage of our lives together. I don't want to stagnate."

"What does he say? When you ask him about a timeline?"

She sighs. "He just keeps saying he's not ready. And that's valid," she hurries to add. "I'm not trying to rush him. But, shit, girl, I'm thirty-two. I want to have kids. I want to be married before we start trying for kids. We've been together for six years. It's like, either he's ready or he will never be ready."

"What does he need from you? In order to get there?"

Rach shrugs. "I'm not sure. He doesn't tell me specifics, just that he's not ready."

I take a hefty sip of my mimosa. She doesn't need my strong, single, not-interested-in-marriage viewpoint right now. She needs support.

Although…

In the last few weeks, things have changed for me. I don't know that I'd necessarily give her the same advice now as I would have done BJ—Before Jared.

It's difficult for me to shift from my single mindset to being in a relationship. I still consider myself to be single, even though I have a committed dating relationship. It's a mindset thing more than anything to me. I'm not *not* committed to Jared. I'm just… in my head, I'm still single.

I've been single for a long time. How do I shift that mindset?

Since Sammy, I haven't been interested in partnering up with anyone. Sure, I have friends. Sure, I have people I partner with for work. But I never had a *romantic* partner.

And now I do.

It's weird having to care about someone else's feelings, to work their schedule into mine. I'm not used to being held accountable to anyone else. My family never really cared to see beyond the surface-level. My friends have always accepted me at face value. Jared sees beyond that. It's disconcerting.

But I really like it. It surprises me how much.

Next week, I have to stand in front of my entire family and introduce him as my boyfriend. That's a level of commitment I don't know that I'm ready for. I haven't even told them I'm bringing someone, half convinced either he—or I—will back out at the last minute.

They say you don't truly know someone until you travel with them. Add in meeting the parents on top of that? Gag me with a spoon. It's my personal idea of hell.

Although we have had some pretty explosive hotel room sex. Maybe that is what I should look forward to. There's something about trying to break a steel bed frame that turns me on like no other. And not having to clean the sheets after? Sign me the fuck up.

Rachel sighs again. "I just want him to put the same effort into the relationship as I am. It's like I do all the emotional labor and he just glides through life on my coattails. Like, why do I have to be the one to remind him to do chores? It's his apartment, too. He should know how to empty the dishwasher and to scrub the fucking toilet."

"Can you increase the housecleaner?" They have a service that comes once a month. I use the same service, actually. I have them set to come biweekly because I do *not* enjoy cleaning.

My friend glares at me. "Who do you think schedules them?"

"Are you happy?" I ask her gently. "Seriously, truly—does he make you happy?"

Rachel sighs. "Yeah. I think so."

"You should know by now."

"I mean, it's been six years."

I want to snap at her. If it's been six years, she has more than enough data to know he's not about to change. She's a scientist, a nuclear physicist. She knows better than to believe anecdotal evidence. Why does she expect it to happen?

Besides, everyone knows that all Eriks with a K are evil. The good ones are the Erics with a C.

"You have to do what you think is right," I finally tell her. "You know I'll be supporting you every step of the way." I stop short of offering her my spare room. I don't think she's ready to hear it.

Rach gives me a watery smile. "Thanks, babe. I don't know what I'd do without you."

The conversation turns to more pleasant topics, like Arielle and Asher's wedding coming up this winter. We're still a good six months away, though Arielle has joked about eloping three separate times in the last three weeks. Her mother is driving her nuts. And speaking of…

"I'm bringing Jared to Arizona," I blurt in the middle of Rachel's sentence about the bridesmaid dresses.

She gapes at me. "Fuck me," she says. "It's serious?"

I shake my head. "No, but I can't show up alone and he's the guy I'm dating, so I invited him."

Her eyes go wide. "You dating anyone at all is still a big deal, babe."

"It makes me itchy," I admit quietly.

Rachel laughs. "You know, there are creams for that."

I waggle my eyebrows. "We got tested. I'm good there."

That was one of Jared's requirements. He's not ready for a vasectomy, and I get it, it's a lot of pressure to put on a new relationship. We're still using condoms and I'm on birth control—can't risk any accidents until Yoni decides if he wants me to have a kid for him—but it was easy to agree to exclusivity once we confirmed we were good and clear. And I don't have to worry if a condom *does* break or I *do* miss a pill.

Plus, the birth control helps regulate my raging PMDD. I honestly don't know how I'd survive without it. I can't go back to having a week of panic attacks every time I ovulate.

"So you're like… really doing this," Rachel says quietly.

I raise my eyebrows. "Doing what?"

"Dating. Putting yourself out there."

I shrug. "Not really. It's casual."

She rolls her eyes. "For you, that's basically announcing your engagement." Her face falls. "I don't know that it'll ever happen for me…"

"It will," I tell her firmly. I don't know when, and I don't know with whom, but I have faith that she'll find the right person for her. I don't think it'll be with Erik.

But I'm not about to tell her that.

twenty-five

. . .

Jared

SADIE CLUTCHES MY ARM. "Please don't let this color what you think about me."

"I'd never," I assure her, squeezing her hand.

"They're not…"

"Hey, I know the real you," I tell her gently. "I've seen it these past few months. I *know* you. These assholes don't."

"They aren't assholes," she mutters under her breath.

I huff out a laugh. "If you say so."

"I do. They're my family." She doesn't sound happy about that; she sounds sullen, resigned.

"They can still be assholes and your family. Doesn't mean you're cut from the same cloth. Just means they got the shit end of the stick."

"You're a shit end of the stick," she retorts.

Her eyes are brighter, though. She doesn't seem nearly as sad.

"So how do you want to play this?" I adjust my tie. "Are we dating or more…?"

She blows out a breath. "We're *not* in a relationship. I told you, I'm not interested—"

I roll my eyes. "Babe, I get it, I'm fucking fantastic in bed. I know *in real life* we are still casual. What do we tell your parents, though?"

"Oh. Um…"

"Haven't thought that far ahead?" I tease.

She tenses up.

"Shit. Sades, you know that's—"

"As far as *they* are concerned, we're dating," she finally says. "We're committed and exclusive. We met through mutual friends. If anyone says shit about getting married, deflect the fuck away."

"Got it. No marriage."

"I don't want to get married to *anyone*," she stresses. "It has nothing to do with you. I'm sure you're the marrying type."

Even though we've discussed this briefly, it doesn't hurt to reiterate how I feel.

I shrug. "Maybe. If the right situation came around. I'm not opposed to life partnership. I just know I don't want the elaborate wedding with the house in the suburbs and 2.5 kids."

In other words… the life her parents—and mine—have always insisted they enjoy. The lives her sisters have fallen into.

Maybe they truly are happy. I don't know. I'm certain I wouldn't be, though.

Sadie sighs. "You're sure you don't? You won't change your mind in six years?"

"Maybe we should have this conversation somewhere other than your parents' doorstep?" I ask mildly.

I've read online that it's a red flag for a man to be in his mid-thirties, unmarried, and no kids. It's not that I don't *want* to be married. For the right woman, I would do it. I almost did for Candace. But for so long, I was focused on myself and my career. And now that I have a steady job and a new place to live, I'm getting settled again… I'm ready to

start dating. I'm coming around to the idea of a relationship.

In theory. If only the person I wanted to be with didn't
think I was prickly scum on the bottom of her shoe.

That seems harsh. Maybe she doesn't think like that, not
anymore. I don't understand some people's ability to utterly
detest someone yet want to have sex with them. So maybe
there's hope for us yet.

But when she clutches at me like I'm her lifeline, panic in
her eyes…

"Do we need to treat this like a scene?" I ask.

She turns to me, her eyebrows raised.

"Do you need ground rules and guidance?"

"You'd do that?"

"I know you well enough that you don't want to be
submissive all the time," I tell her. "Every now and then…
right now, I think you need to let go. So let me take it on. Let
me be the one to direct."

She melts. "Thank you. I—thank you."

I squeeze her hand. "What you're going to do is open the
door and introduce me to the people you want me to meet.
The moment they start asking uncomfortable questions, you
deflect to me. I'll handle it. If you need some air, pull on your
earlobe, I'll get you out of there."

She takes a deep breath.

"And after this shit-tastic party is over," I continue, "We'll
go back to the hotel and I'll fuck you until you melt into a
puddle. Sounds good?"

Sadie swallows. "Yes. I think."

The front door is unlocked, and the door swings open to
reveal a tightly packed crowd. There's got to be wall-to-wall
people in here.

"Sadie. You're here," an older woman says with no inflec-
tion in her tone. She looks her up and down with a faint
sneer. "You've gained weight."

As Sadie bit her lip, I tug on her hand. "Come on, babe, let's go introduce me to your friends and family."

"This is my grandmother, Myrna Hershkowitz." Her voice is quiet, a far cry from her usual robust exuberance.

"And who are you?" Myrna turns her disapproving gaze on me.

Luckily, I don't give two shits about what the old crone thinks of me. What does bother me is the way Sadie shrunk into herself.

"Jared Aviyente." I don't smile or offer her my hand, and her lips purse at what she no doubt sees as a slight. It may be bad manners. She doesn't deserve my respect.

Myrna harrumphs. She opens her mouth to give me a piece of her mind.

I squeeze Sadie's hand. "Let's mingle."

She opens her mouth, no doubt feeling the need to kowtow to her family's matriarch.

"I could use some water."

With the gentle prompting, she seems to reboot and recalibrate. Her hand in mine, she pulls me deeper into the party without a further word to her grandmother.

We get about ten feet in when we are approached by a woman with the same voluptuous frame and wavy hair as my girlfriend, her face round and pink.

"Sades. Hey," she says, reaching out and squeezing her shoulder. "You look good."

"Thanks," Sadie says stiffly.

Why is her family so fixated on her looks?

Yes, she's gorgeous, but that is in no way the most interesting thing about her.

"This is Jared," she says as an afterthought. "J, this is my sister, Sarah."

"Nice to meet you." For the sister, I pull out my manners, offering my hand to shake.

Sarah's grip is firm. "I didn't know you were seeing anyone."

"Why would you?" Sadie's voice shakes. "It's not like you've ever asked a single question about my life."

Sarah inhales sharply. "I'm sorry you feel that way."

Sadie shakes out her shoulders. "I'm sorry. I'm in a shitty mood. You don't deserve that."

"We haven't been dating long," I offer.

"Long enough to come to this party together," Sarah says slowly.

"When you know, you know." Even though I try to keep my response glib, deep in my chest, I know the truth.

I do know.

I like Sadie. A lot. But as much as I might want more, I know she's like a skittish kitten. One wrong move and I'll scare her off—for good.

So I can be patient. I can wait until she's ready to hear what I want to say. I can give her the time to get to where I am.

Sarah offers me a smile. "I'd love to get to know you more. Are you guys sticking around?"

"We fly back tomorrow afternoon," Sadie says. "The bookstore doesn't give me a lot of time off."

Carefully, I hold back my laugh. She's in charge of the schedule. She could easily arrange for a week or more of time off. She has no problems doing so when she has a book signing or is under a deadline crunch.

When it comes to taking actual time off for personal reasons? It would be more likely to find a thunderstorm in the Negev.

Sarah's lips purse. "You're still working at the bookstore?"

I'm not sure if her family knows she's the manager of the store or think she's a low-level lackey. They definitely don't know about Sylvie. She's said multiple times they wouldn't understand.

The longer I stand here, the more I get it.

Family is more than blood relation. I'm lucky that Yoni and I get along with our parents. They support us, they drive us crazy, but at the end of the day, I can trust that they genuinely want what's best for us.

I don't know that I could say the same about the Hershkowitzs.

Sadie's posture is stiff as she introduces me to various cousins and family friends. She steers clear from mentioning either of our professions. I don't know if it's because I'm currently in a career transition or so she won't have to hear the condescension about her chosen career path.

These people aren't her people. She's made it clear she's here because she feels the obligation, not because she wants to be. She keeps her contact with them as minimal as possible. I get it. If I was constantly derided for what I look like, who I date, and what kind of job I work, I'd be uninterested in spending any more time with them than absolutely necessary.

Sadie's other sisters look like her, too. Talia seems genuinely nice. Tamar… Well, if I hadn't already heard from Yoni how much of a cunt she is, I probably would have come to the same conclusion within five minutes of meeting her.

The only people I haven't met? Sadie's parents.

"Is this the house you grew up in?" I ask as we skirt past the bathroom line to the kitchen.

She nods, chewing on her lip.

"Show me your room?"

Her eyes go wide. "We can't fool around here."

"Who said anything about fooling around?" Although normally I'd be down for some semi-public sex, the thought of putting her through that so close to people she doesn't get along with makes my stomach turn. All they'd do is judge her. That's not sexy.

Sadie takes me by the hand, pulling me up the flight of

stairs to a small, tucked away room at the end of a long hallway.

"They put Baby in a corner?" I ask lightly.

"I'm the youngest." She shrugs. "At least I had a room to myself. Sarah and Talia had to share."

The walls are pink. Bright pink. The carpet is an old and dingy blue. A daybed is in the corner, fluffy white comforter half-hiding the trundle underneath. A small desk is in the corner with a child's size chair. A chest of toys is overflowing with Barbies, magnetic tiles, Legos, and trucks.

Sadie stares at the room, her eyes wide.

"What's wrong?" I tighten my grip on her hand and am gratified when she doesn't immediately pull away from the support I'm offering.

"This is *not* what it looked like last time I was here." She sits heavily on the daybed. "I didn't expect them to keep everything the same, I haven't lived here in years, but I didn't realize..."

"They didn't tell you they changed it?"

She shakes her head. "Not like they tell me much to begin with."

The pain in her voice is audible.

Sitting beside her, I draw her hand into my lap, running my thumb over the tendons on the back of her hand.

"Do you want a distraction?"

She looks up at me, hesitation on her face.

"Clothes will stay on," I add.

Nodding readily, she sets her hand high on my thigh. "I could..."

Her submission would distract her.

But as much as I want to direct, to control her pleasure, I know this isn't the right time or place.

Tangling my hand in her curls, I kiss her with insistent pressure, taking control. She lets out a soft sigh, her eyes fluttering closed.

My hand moves to her neck, resting gently along the column of her throat, my thumb in the hollow of her clavicle. She lets out a loud moan I hurry to smother.

Her strong, supple body yields for me. We have a routine now, a familiarity with each other. I know what her sounds mean, when she's completely lost to pleasure or when she needs more attention to get there.

She's wearing a brushed velvet jumpsuit, the kind of sensitive material that will show every crease and crinkle in the fabric and only has one way to take it on or off. It looks great on her, showcasing her curves and making her ass pop. Right now, I wish it was on the floor.

Her breathy sighs go straight to my cock, making it chub up in my suit pants. I shift on the bed to relieve some of the pressure. Sadie crawls up after me, straddling my lap. She hovers, not ready to put her weight on my lap.

She doesn't understand how much I need it. Need *her*.

My hands on her hips, I yank her down to my lap. She lets out a soft pant when she feels the hard ridge of my dick pressed right up against her center, grinding down on me.

Breathing hard, Sadie pulls my hand off her hip and drags it back up to her neck. I flex my fingers. Her mouth falls open in a silent O, her eyes fluttering shut.

"Jared…"

She doesn't use my name in bed often. I don't know if it's a conscious thing or not. Maybe it's because of the way we started, anonymous and discreet. Either way, the use of my name now sends a lightning bolt of desire through me.

There's a thundering sound, and then the bedroom door crashes open.

Immediately, I yank Sadie down onto my lap, wrapping my arms around her to protect her from the intruders.

It's a gaggle of kids, ranging in age from baby to preteen, chaperoned by one of the sisters. I don't remember which of the three it is.

A little girl—maybe three or four years old—stares at us.

"Aunt Sadie! What are you doing?"

"Hi." She waves awkwardly at the kids. "I didn't know this was a playroom."

The kids descend on the toys in the corner. The preteen pulls out a phone and drops onto the beanbag chair.

Her sister sneers. "I'm sure."

Tamar. That's it. Even though I didn't study the family tree, I've heard enough from both Sadie and Yoni to know this is the bitchy sister. She seems to take it personally that Sadie is out living her best life while she's trapped in a life she hates.

It doesn't help that for a while, they lived together when Sadie first moved to Boston. Tamar went to Newton State College in the Boston suburbs and moved to the city after graduation. Sadie managed to share a space with her older sister for six whole weeks before she moved out of the condo their parents had bought and into a sketchy share house on the bad side of town.

Tamar took it personally. Even when she moved back to Scottsdale a few months later, for whatever reason, she maintained the grudge. Even now, she's cold and aloof.

Sadie squeezes my hand. "We should go."

"Yeah, that's probably best," Tamar snipes.

I roll my eyes. Her tangible frustration is adorably petty. If she would just let it go like Elsa, she would be so much happier.

Standing, I straighten my clothes as Sadie does the same, then immediately reach for her hand.

Her hand is shaking. I squeeze, and she relaxes, letting me lead. The kids are ignoring us, more absorbed by the toys than by any grown-up drama.

As we descend the giant staircase, I can feel eyes on us. Sadie seems to shrink, hiding behind me. I keep my hold on her firm and sure. I'm not going to back out. I'm not going to change my mind.

The strong, vibrant woman I've known the last few weeks is nowhere to be found. It's devastating that her family has such a stronghold on her. They don't deserve her. They don't treat her well.

Still, I can't fault her for not giving them up quite yet. When they're all she's ever known, when all the media she consumes tells her they're the only ones who are going to love her, when everything points to a lifetime of just barely having her needs met…

It makes sense. A deeper part of her recognizes her parents will never love her the way she wants, so she writes happily ever afters where the families *do* treat their loved ones that way. She thought she'd never find a romantic partner of her own, so she writes love stories to experience some of their love, too.

I'll spend the rest of my life proving to her that she is worthy of love. Yoni, her friends… it won't be hard to convince them. We love her. We want the best for her—the actual best, not just the perfunctory mediocre baseline her family is partial to.

twenty-six

. . .

Sadie

"FUCK, YOU'RE GORGEOUS," Jared says. His hand is wrapped around my throat, exerting the barest hint of pressure.

I'm laid bare in front of him, my wild mess of waves splayed on the hotel room pillow, my naked body his to enjoy. My hands are restrained above my head, tied off with silk ropes, and he settles between my thighs.

"I could do this every day for the rest of my life," he says quietly, his thumb dipping into the hollow of my throat.

Swallowing, I bring my eyes to his. His rich amber eyes are dark and bright, filled with an emotion I can't identify.

"Every fucking day," Jared says firmly.

The heavy weight of his promise hangs between us.

"Don't say that." Even though I mean to be strong, my voice comes out in a whisper. "Don't promise things you don't mean."

He leans over me, brushing my lips with his in the softest kiss.

"I do, though."

"But…"

We're supposed to be keeping things casual. Easy. No strings.

"It's okay if you're not ready," he says. He squeezes my hip in reassurance. "We'll take it one day at a time."

Nodding, I try to decide if I'm okay with that.

He's been by my side all day. He stared down my cunt of a grandmother and dressed down my bitchy sister, stood by me when the non-bitchy ones asked insensitive questions about my life. We managed to expertly avoid my parents, only saying hello when they were in the midst of conversations with other people, so we wouldn't have to stop and do the whole "introduction to the boyfriend" spiel. He knew exactly how to flatter and disarm my cousins and aunts, how to get my uncles to talk about anything other than baseball, and was great with all of the uptight friends ready to cast aspersions on my character.

He's been perfect.

And when I think about coming back here, I'm already dreading doing it without him. How could I do this alone?

No, not alone. Even if I had someone by my side, Yoni or Arielle or Rachel or Ceci, it wouldn't be the same. I don't know that there's *anyone* else on the planet I would rather do this with.

"Maybe…"

He lifts an eyebrow, no judgment on his face.

"Maybe we try it two days at a time," I offer. "Just two."

Jared's smile stretches from ear to ear. "Yeah. Two days sounds great."

He covers my body with his, his knees digging into the mattress so his heavy bulk isn't directly on top of me. Usually I like it, especially after he brings me to orgasm more than three times in a row and I'm a boneless, sated pile of goo. When my arms are restrained, though, I need the respite.

His bearded cheek nestles into the curve of my neck, kissing the column of my throat. I tilt my head to give him more access and he nuzzles into me. He's careful not to leave any marks. A little beard burn is okay, though I like it better between my thighs, but when I have to be around my family…

They don't know me. They think I'm still the old version of me, quiet and demure. I don't have the freedom to be myself, loud and opinionated.

In Boston, I don't care what people think of me. Why does a stranger's opinion matter? And my friends already love me for who I am—they don't think less of me for liking sex.

But my parents…

Jared pinches my arm. "Hey. I'm doing my best work here."

With a sigh, I lean into him. "I know. I'm sor—"

He covers my mouth with his hand. "I don't want to hear that word."

My brow arches.

"You do not have to apologize. You have a lot on your mind."

Deflated, I nod. "Yeah."

He studies me, his forehead crinkled as he takes me in. He's assessing me, but he isn't critiquing. He's frowning, but I already know he's not upset with me.

To my surprise, Jared reaches for the tie between my hands and pulls it free.

"Change of plans," he announces.

"Oh?" I pull my hands free from the silk ties and flex my wrists.

He hauls me off the bed and then settles me on his lap. I move to straddle him and he manipulates me until he has me the way he wants me, laying on my belly across his thighs.

Jared's hand trails over the curve of my ass, his fingertips digging into the firm flesh.

"I'm going to spank you now," he says.

He's a pleasure Dom; he wants to bring me pleasure. At

the same time, he knows when I need to get out of my head. We haven't gone there yet, but we've discussed it, and we've established parameters for what it means. I don't want to be punished. I don't want to be made to feel inferior. If he thinks a spanking will get me back into the heat of the moment...

I want to please him.

He wants to bring me pleasure, but I want to please him just as much. If he thinks this is what I need, I'll give it a try. I'll be a good girl.

I'll be *his* good girl.

His voice is hoarse, his breathing ragged. I can feel the hard ridge of him beneath my belly and I wiggle against him.

"Nope." He gathers my wrists again, holding them over my head, while his other hand caresses my spine. "You need to behave."

"Or what?" I turn to look over my shoulder at him, a teasing smile on my lips. Fuck, I love challenging him—and he likes it, too, if the gleam in his eye is any indication.

He trails a finger up the seam of my legs. I'm wet, the slickness there a taunting promise of what's to come.

Hopefully, me.

My thighs shake and he smirks. As I spread my legs, he presses a finger inside me, and the slow stretch makes my eyes roll back into my head. He fucks me with shallow thrusts, not giving me the pressure or pleasure I need, just enough to warm me up.

I rest my cheek on the bed, my back arched, my hips up.

Jared withdraws his finger from within me. I don't have time to mourn the loss before a loud crack echoes throughout the room.

And then I feel it, the blooming burn spreading from where his hand made contact with my ass.

I jolt, my hips snapping up.

His hand settles on the small of my back, pressing lightly, and the contact grounds me.

"You're okay," he murmurs. His fingertips trace small circles on my back.

Relaxing, I consciously release the tension in my body.

"There we go." His voice is soft, comforting.

And then he spanks me again.

And again.

The contrast of his sharp, cracking smacks and the soft way he caresses me in between is doing funny things to my brain. It's hovering just out of reach, taunting me, tantalizing.

I want it so bad.

Sub-space.

It's that floaty feeling when the endorphins hit and everything feels good. Jared doesn't send me there every time, but when he does…

I want it. I *need* it.

"You're doing so well," he says. His voice sounds far away. "You're taking this so well."

I can feel the impact of his hand against my ass, but the sensation is muted, the blooming burn fading into a warm glow.

Jared's hand teases between my legs, gathering the wetness before he slides two fingers inside of me. Every sensation is heightened, every nerve in my body alive and humming.

He sets a rough pace, fingering me quickly. Just as I start to really get into the groove, he pulls his fingers out and spanks me again.

I come alive, pleasure blooming from deep within me.

"That's it, baby." He slips his fingers through my crack, dragging the wetness there. My hole clenches, wanting him there, everywhere. "You're doing so good."

"Please." My voice comes out muffled by the bedspread. "Please, sir."

His fingers thrust inside of me and I nearly explode.

There's added pressure as he adds a third finger, stretching me as far as I like. Fisting is a no-go for me.

When he releases my wrists, I pause for a second, unsure. And then he's helping me onto my hands and knees.

"Fuck yourself on my fingers, baby," Jared says. "Take what you need."

With the added leverage, I arch my back and do as he says, taking his fingers deep inside me.

He brushes some hair out of my face. The tender sweetness in his eyes contrasted with the filthy way he's fingering me makes me clench around him.

"That's it," he murmurs. "You're doing so good."

And it's the praise that sends me tumbling over the edge. Pleasure courses through my veins, coalescing into a ball of fire deep within me. My vision goes black and my arms give out and I collapse onto his lap.

When I come to a few minutes later, I'm laying in the bed under the covers, Jared's warm body wrapped around me.

In his arms, I feel safe. Protected. Cherished.

"How're you doing?" he murmurs, his arm heavy around my back.

I assess rather than give him a glib answer.

"My ass is kind of sore."

"I'll get you some aloe," Jared says. He runs his hand through my hair. "Other than that?"

"I feel good. Loose." I wiggle my arms a little, trapped as they are against his chest. My thoughts aren't heavy anymore. I feel like I can breathe again.

His soft smile makes me glow inside. "I'm glad."

"Did you come?"

He shakes his head. "It's not about that."

"But—"

Leaning down, he gives me a soft kiss. "Your needs are more important than my wants."

I open my mouth to argue.

"Bringing you pleasure gives me pleasure," he says. "You did so good."

There's that warm glow again. "I did?"

Nodding, he brushes his nose against mine. "You did. You took it beautifully."

I beam. I'm a sucker for his praise.

"Come on," Jared says. "Let me get some lotion for you, and then I'll feed you a snack, and then I'll hold you a little."

"I'm fine."

"Aftercare is important," he says gently. "It's for me as much as it is for you. Please, let me do this."

I melt. "Okay."

His smile stretches from ear to ear. "I'm really glad we're doing this."

Somehow, I don't think he just means aftercare.

And where usually that might scare me... I think I'm coming around to the idea.

twenty-seven

. . .

Jared

SUNDAY BRUNCH with the Hershkowitz family was not high on my list of things to do while in Scottsdale. It's not like we could conceivably say no, though. We traveled all this way to see the family. The least we could do, Bubbie Myrna sniped, was sit down for a meal.

Sadie is practically shaking as we get out of the ride-share. She doesn't want to be here. As much as I'm not looking forward to it, I know my job is to support her.

So I will.

Taking her hand in mine, I kiss the back of her knuckles. She gives me a faint smile, distracted.

"Hey."

She looks over at me, focusing on my gaze. "Yeah?"

"We've got this. We can do this," I tell her firmly. "I've got your back."

This time, her smile is more genuine. "I don't deserve you."

"Or me, you." I shake my head. "Good thing we're not keeping score."

"We're not?" she jokes as she rings the bell. "I thought it was a competition."

"Nah. The only competition is how many orgasms I can give—oh, hello," I cut off abruptly as the door opens.

Sarah, the second eldest sister, is staring with wide eyes. "Hi," she says, a bit woodenly. She shakes her head as if to clear her mind. "You know you don't need to ring the bell."

Sadie shrugs. "I don't live here."

Her sister's eyes fall. "I suppose not."

Sarah is a few years older than me at thirty-four. She's a pharmacist at the local hospital and has two kids, a girl who's four and a boy who is almost two. She was the nicest of the three sisters I met yesterday.

Not that Talia wasn't nice. She was *fine*, just a little boring. Then again, she's a lawyer. They're usually pretty boring. She has three kids—an infant plus two in school. I don't know their ages because she didn't tell me and, frankly, I didn't care enough to ask. They're young.

Tamar was the sister that accosted us in Sadie's former bedroom. Can't say I've been eager to talk to her.

Mr. and Mrs. Hershkowitz seem… average. He's a Pharm.D. and a professor at the local pharmacy college. She owns an enormous catering business. Based on the spread yesterday, she does fairly well for herself.

Mrs. Hershkowitz is sitting in the armchair holding a baby. I think it's Talia's kid, based on how small it is. I don't know baby size or age milestones. None of my friends in Denver had kids, and the people I've met in Boston aren't in a baby stage of life quite yet. The only time I see kids is online when I keep up with my old college friends. It's a little weird that I've never met the children but I know how old they are and read about all the trials and tribulations of raising them.

It just cements my desire not to have children. I'm sure they're fine. When Yoni has a kid, I know I'll love it. It's not a lifestyle I want for myself. Especially if I get another job that requires me to be on the road for six months of the year, the last thing I want is to virtually abandon my child for the sake of my career. That's not cool. It's only setting them up for abandonment issues.

It's bad enough that I'll have to leave my partner for all those trips. Sadie, I believe her when she says it'll work for her lifestyle. She wants space. She wants independence. My being on the road will give her enough alone time that she can decompress between writing her books, working at the bookstore, and all her travel.

Mr. Hershowkitz comes into the room, his big walrus mustache twitching with dissatisfaction. I think that's his default setting.

"So you decided to join us," he says loudly.

Sadie flinches. "We got caught in traffic."

We're only a few minutes later than anticipated. Hardly enough to get upset over.

"Come, sit," Mrs. Hershkowitz says. "I want to meet your boyfriend."

A little boy grins. "Aunt Sadie has a *boyfriend.*"

She sits on the empty loveseat and I sit close beside her, setting my hand on her knee automatically. It's how we sit on the couch at her place when we watch *The West Wing* every night. Well, usually we're naked, and usually my hand isn't exactly on her knee—a little higher.

I'm about to take away my hand when she sets hers on top of mine, leaning into me.

"Mom, this is Jared," Sadie says.

"Nice to meet you, ma'am," I say. "Properly, that is."

She nods at me, her flinty brown eyes studying me. "What is it you do?"

Great. She dove right in for the kill.

"I work in hockey. Right now I'm working in the Logistics department for the Grizzlies," I tell her, matter of fact.

"I like hockey," Sarah says.

"Me, too," Sadie says quietly. "My friend works for the team, too. A group of us like to go to the games."

"Is that how you met?" Talia asks, waggling a finger between us. "At a game?"

I shake my head. "She works with my brother. He set us up."

Let them think Yoni works at the bookstore. If they don't know about Sylvie, I'm not about to spoil her secret.

It's Sadie's prerogative who she tells about her Sylvie persona. I don't blame her for not sharing it with her family; they've proven to be woefully unsupportive in the rest of her life, I highly doubt they'd be allies to her writing career.

"And where are you from?" Bubbie Myrna asks.

"I'm from Tacoma," I reply, squeezing Sadie's knee.

"No, but where are you *from*?"

Oh.

She's asking why I'm brown.

"My family is Israeli."

Myrna raises her eyebrows. Most modern Israelis are transplants from another country, at least prior to 1948 when they could finally return to the homeland.

"I have family from Spain, Morocco, and Greece," I finally say. "My grandmother's family settled in Israel, then she brought my dad here when he was a kid."

Mr. Hershkowitz squints at me. "They left Israel?" Not many people leave the promised land, especially not for the U.S.

"My grandmother worked for the embassy. Moved back when my dad was in college."

I don't explain my mother's immigration story. Her family left Morocco for Gibraltar, then immigrated to Israel. Their families lived a few neighborhoods apart, but they didn't meet until they were in the U.S. for college.

My grandmother passed when I was in middle school. She was a genuinely kind soul. When we'd visit her apartment in Haifa, she'd take me down to the markets and let me pick anything I wanted from the street vendors. Some of the best summers of my life were spent in Israel in her little apartment.

My parents Anglicized our names given that we were being raised in the U.S. Besides, they had enough difficulty with their own "ethnic" names in the 70s. I'm grateful they gave us the option to assimilate, even though I wish it wasn't a decision they had to make.

My brother chose to go by his Hebrew name, Yonatan, whereas I kept the Anglicized name of Jared. My grandmother always spoke to us in Hebrew, my parents only occasionally spoke it when they wanted to have a conversation they didn't want us to be privy to. I've lost most of the language now, given that I haven't spoken it in about twenty years, but I remember a few choice phrases. I know enough to call my brother all sorts of bad names, order off a menu, ask for the bathroom, and explain that I don't speak Hebrew.

The inquisition continues. Where did I go to college? What did I study? Why did I go into broadcast journalism?

Fuck, I'm surprised they haven't asked why I'm not married yet.

"Is it serious?" Mrs. Hershkowitz waves between us. "Any plans to go ring shopping?"

… and there it is.

"I'm not interested in getting married," Sadie says quietly.

I squeeze her knee. "Me, either."

Her mother blinks. "Why not?"

She shrugs. "Not something I'm interested in."

"I suppose there's no need anymore," Myrna snipes. "Why buy the cow when he can get the milk for free?"

My eyes narrow. "Excuse me?"

"My views on marriage have nothing to do with Jared and everything to do with me," Sadie says firmly. "It's not something I want to pursue for myself."

"So you'll die alone?"

"Maybe." She lifts a shoulder in what I can tell is forced

ambivalence. "Rather die alone and happy than miserable with someone I can't stand."

Sarah chokes.

Mrs. Hershkowitz frowns. "Your father is my best friend."

Sadie blinks innocently. "Oh, I'm not talking about you. I'm sure you guys are happy. I mean, wow, forty years without killing each other. That's something to be proud of."

From what she's told me, her parents live mostly separate lives. Her father is busy with the college and the golf course, and her mother has the business and her volunteering plus babysitting the myriad grandchildren. It doesn't leave them a lot of time for each other.

She mentioned she didn't think it occurred to them it even was an option to divorce. They aren't particularly nice to each other, more resentful than happy. But people in their social circle don't divorce; they simply live unhappily ever after until one of them dies.

I don't want that life for myself. Neither does Sadie. If we last the forty years, great. If we don't... at least we can untangle and separate without dealing with lawyers.

Hopefully.

I'm not thinking about separation, though. It's early days, but I can already see us going the distance. If she decides down the line she wants a ring, I'll happily get one for her. As long as she's happy with me, I'm happy. That's all I care about.

Mr. Hershkowitz clears his throat loudly. "Let's eat."

The caterers have prepared a bagel brunch. It's traditional Ashkenazi fare. The table is overflowing with bagels and shmear, lox and herring, whitefish salad and tuna salad, and veggie crudités. There's enough food to feed fifty people.

It's *very* different from the way my family does food. That doesn't mean it's wrong. It's just different. My family's cuisine reflects our Middle Eastern heritage, whereas theirs reflects Eastern European. We're both Jewish, just two different sides of the same coin.

Sadie picks at half of an everything bagel. She warned me she usually didn't have a great appetite around her family and that we'd have to find alternative snacks en route to the airport this afternoon.

Sarah puts a bagel on her plate and Myrna immediately fusses at her. "You don't need all that," she says, trying to take the plate out of her hand. "Why don't you have some fruit?"

"I'm good, thanks," Sarah says firmly. She goes heavy on the cream cheese, adding lox and capers.

Tamar has a plate of fruit and is nibbling at a slice of cheese. Talia is digging into the whitefish salad.

The commentary doesn't stop there. Myrna comments on the grandchildren's messy table manners—hello, they're *children*—and Mrs. Hershkowitz has nothing nice to say about Tamar's outfit.

What surprises me most is that the sisters just sit there and *take it*. They let their parents and grandmother degrade and insult them. They let them criticize every single thing they do.

Sadie is a sad, quiet shell of herself. The exuberant, effervescent woman I care about is a shadow around her family. How sad that the people who should love her most are the quickest to cut her down.

My watch buzzes. We have six hours until our flight takes off.

"We should get going," I announce, even though we have plenty of time. I don't exactly want to wait at the airport for six hours. But I have to get Sadie out of here.

We gather our things and say goodbye. There are a lot of empty promises to get together again soon and keep in touch. I know neither party wants to do so, but they both probably feel like it's required.

Sarah pulls me aside. "It was nice to meet you, Jared," she says, and I think she's being sincere. "You're good for her."

"Oh?"

"I've never seen her as happy as she is with you." Her eyes are sad. "I want her to be happy. It's clear being here is making it worse."

"She's comfortable in Boston," I finally say.

Sarah squeezes my arm. "Take care of her. Will you?"

A lump in my throat, I nod. "I'm doing my best."

twenty-eight

. . .

Sadie

THE QUEBEC SUNSHINE beats down on the sunroom windows, making the temperature rise in the otherwise cool house my friends and I have rented for the week.

LuAnn, Rosemary, Andie, and I try to do this at least once a year. We all have projects to work on—I'm knee deep in final edits for my current Work In Progress—and the goal of the week is to Get Work Done. This trip has been booked for six months.

So I am *not* thinking about Jared, back in Boston, splayed out in my bed and looking adorably rumpled when I left for the airport at ass o'clock in the morning yesterday. Technically he still lives with Yoni, though he only sleeps there once a week and is in my bed the rest of the time. Now that the hockey season is over, his days at the office are shorter, but his free time is full of job applications.

I don't want him to move in. It's too soon. But he can't move out into an apartment of his own until he has a real job. Jacky's on maternity leave for a few more months, but eventually, she'll come back. We all know this is temporary.

So why am I tossing and turning every night that I'm alone in my bed?

I've never liked to have someone sleep in the same bed with me—I'm a light sleeper and every shift and sound wakes me up. Somehow, having Jared's warm body beside mine is a comfort, even when we're not touching. The steady snuffle of his breathing works better to lull me asleep than any white noise machine I've ever tried. And the morning sex basically whenever I want? Yeah, that's not bad, either.

Actually moving in together? Combining our lives? Commingling finances? That feels waaaay too soon for a casual dating situation-ship with a guy I couldn't stand three months ago.

If the end goal isn't marriage, what is it? What are we working toward?

"Holy hell on a Cheez-It," LuAnn says. "Your thoughts are so loud, you're giving *me* anxiety."

We're sitting across from each other at the kitchen table, working on our own projects. Rosemary is taking a much-needed shower break. Andie's walking around the neighborhood, dictating smut into her phone. And I…

I am seriously wigging out.

"I think I'm broken," I tell Lu.

She rolls her eyes. "You are *not* broken."

"Okay, fine. Defective, then."

Lu heaves a sigh. "Don't make me get up out of my chair to spank you."

"Careful, I might like it," I tease, and inevitably, my thoughts immediately go to Jared.

He hasn't spanked me again. That night in Scottsdale, I needed it to get out of my head. I was so wound up—and he knew exactly how to fix that. It's like he's a mind-reader or something.

Or maybe he just knows *me*.

"You're thinking about the boy again," Lu says, rolling her eyes again.

"Yeah," I admit. My voice is quiet. This is supposed to be a girls' trip. No, a working trip. A working girls' trip.

"You haven't had this before."

I shake my head. "My last relationship was back in college."

"Sometimes I forget how much younger you are than me." Lu says it with a smile tinged with sadness.

"I mean, I've been with other guys," I hurry to add. "There was never any commitment or feelings or anything. It was always just sex."

"And now there's feelings?" She raises her eyebrows.

"I don't know."

She laughs. "You know how this works."

"I do?"

"Think back to all of your books. The character needs a bit of prodding to realize they're in love."

"It's not that," I'm quick to assure her.

She blinks at me.

"I just… I *like* him."

"You're kind of supposed to like the guy you're shacking up with," Lu teases.

"We're not shacking up. We're just…"

She laughs. "Babe. He's at your house every day."

She would know. He's in the background of our daily video chats nearly every day as he gets ready for work.

"He doesn't live with me. He still lives with Yoni."

My statement rings hollow. He might get his mail at his brother's house, but for all intents and purposes, he lives with me. He just hasn't *moved in* yet.

"You care about him."

My throat tightens. "I do." The words are quiet. "I like him a lot."

"So what's the holdup?"

"I just don't know what happens next," I tell her.

Lu blinks at me. "You get railed into next week by a hottie Pleasure Dom?"

My cheeks heat. "Aside from that."

"What else is there?"

"I mean… I don't want kids. Neither does he," I add. "And neither of us wants to get married. So what do we do?"

"You live your fucking life." LuAnn reaches for my arm, squeezing. "You enjoy the happiness. We're all so caught up in this fairytale of Happy Ever After we forget to live in the here and now."

"The fairytale is our lives' work. It's literally what we're doing right now." I wave my arm at the manuscript in front of me.

"That's not what I'm talking about." She rolls her eyes. "The fairytale is the neat time skip where he doesn't forget to hang up towels and you magically never get PMS and there isn't any conflict, it just rushes to a wedding and babies. The fairytale ignores the real life stuff that happens in everyone's lives. Like one of you being a blanket hog. Or trouble with the in-laws, because everyone's extended family isn't magical and perfect. It's one person being a saver and the other a spender. It's sex droughts and communication and *work*."

"You make it sound so appealing," I tell her dryly.

"There's good, too," she says.

"Like what?"

"Like spending your life with a person who understands you and wants the best for you. Having someone to rely on when things get tough. A person to celebrate the milestones with. Growing old with someone. Entwining your lives, so your family is his and his is yours—the family members you want to claim, that is. It's shared vacations and memories and accidentally using each other's toothbrush. Having someone in your corner."

"I want that." My voice shakes. "Maybe not the toothbrush part, but the rest of it, I really want that."

"And do you think Jared could be that person for you?" she prods.

My heart stops.

Lu pokes me where it hurts.

"Do you think you can be that person *for him*?"

"I want to be."

Why couldn't I have had this realization when we were together? Being on a girls' work trip is horribly inconvenient, but damn it, I have shit to do, and I can't put my entire life on hold just because I suddenly realize I'm in love with the fucker.

Fuck.

I'm in love with him.

That was *not* part of the deal. This was *not* supposed to happen. Guess I've got to go buy a lottery ticket; the impossible actually is possible now.

This was supposed to be casual. No feelings. What the hell is he going to say when I turn the tables on him? This wasn't what we agreed to.

But if there's one thing he's made clear, it's that consent is compulsory. We both have to be into it, or it's not happening.

And it's not fair to him to change the game. If I'm having feelings, he needs to know. He can't consent to casual-with-feelings or anything else if he doesn't know about it.

Although I think the very definition of casual-with-feelings is that R word I've been avoiding for my entire life.

I can't say it. Even to myself, I can't conceptualize the idea of loving someone and having those feelings reciprocated.

It's not "who could ever love me" or even "nobody loves me." It's just so unfathomable to believe that someone actually *wants* to love me. Nobody has ever said those words to me and meant it. Not the way my characters do.

Not the way I want them to.

"I—I need to go." I scramble for my manuscript, shoving the papers into an orderly pile.

"Go where?"

"Boston. I have to—I need to get to Jared. I have to tell him I love him before—"

LuAnn rolls her eyes, but she can't hide her smile. "I'm proud of you, babe. You said the words."

"I have to tell him," I repeat. "I have to go."

We're here for two more days. I can't stand being away from him that long. I—I can't. I won't survive it.

She laughs. "Okay, dumb-dumb. I'll let you go home one day early. Leave the rest of us to die in the wilderness."

It's my turn to roll my eyes. "The wilderness?"

We're in a river-front house in Quebec City, two streets off the main road. There's a Tim Horton's in walking distance. It's hardly the backroads of the Canadian frontier.

She grins. "But first, sit down and finish your damn book," Lu says sternly. "You're almost there. Only a little bit more to go."

twenty-nine

. . .

Jared

WE NEED TO TALK, Sadie's texted. A second message came through immediately after the first. *Nothing is wrong, everything is fine. I just really miss you.*

Once my initial panic passed, I was able to reply that I missed her, too, and I'd see her soon.

Only two more days until she comes home.

Only two more days to decide what I want to do.

I wasn't expecting the email.

We'd like to offer you a position as in-studio regional sports broadcaster for the Big Ten Network, they'd written. *You would cover the conference's hockey matches and daily news updates.*

It's not my dream job. It's not something I applied for.

But it gets me to where I want to be.

The problem? The studio is based in Chicago.

And so when my two days are up, I find myself at the airport, holding a giant poster with her name on it and a bouquet of her favorite flowers. Her plan is to take the T back to the house since I'm supposed to be getting the place ready.

The house is already cleaned and organized. I was able to take care of that earlier today while I waited.

And waited.

And waited.

Hundreds of people pass by. Her flight has landed. She should be here. Where is she??

Finally, I catch sight of her mess of wavy hair. She's wearing one of my Grizzlies sweatshirts, the material hanging off her shoulder. Her phone is held to her ear.

My phone buzzes in my pocket with an incoming call. I ignore it.

She passes right by me, not seeing me.

"Sadie!" I call out.

Her steps falter.

I call her name again.

And I know the moment she sees me, because my heart contracts like there's a fist around my organs, holding on for dear life.

What am I doing? What if she doesn't want this?

Sadie rushes toward me. With a millisecond to spare, I drop the poster and flowers to the floor as she leaps into my arms.

Staggering back a few paces, I wrap my arms around her and breathe her in. Even with the lingering scent of eau de airplane, I can still smell her sweet perfume, and the familiar warmth of it sends tingles all the way down to my toes.

I'm fucking crazy about this woman.

"What are you doing here?" Sadie demands.

"I wanted to see you."

Half-laughing, she scratches her nails through my short beard, and I lean into the contact. "I would be home in an hour."

"I couldn't wait that long," I admit.

Dipping my head, I kiss her, telling her all the things I want to say but can't yet verbalize without her running away. This isn't something I could say over a video chat. This has to be done face to face.

I don't want to run. I don't want *her* to run, either.

I can't control her, though. And if she's not ready to hear it, I won't push. I'll be here when she's ready.

I'm not going anywhere—not without her. She doesn't want to leave. I don't want to leave her. If that means staying in Boston, that's what I'll do. I'm good with that as long as I have her.

"I got a job offer," I tell her.

"You did?" She beams. "Jare, that's—"

"In Chicago."

Her face falls. "Oh. So you're leaving?"

Shaking my head, I trail my thumb over her cheek. "I turned them down."

"What? No! You have to take it. You have to call them and—"

"I don't want it," I tell her firmly. "Not if it means leaving you."

Sadie's eyes widen. "But…"

"I don't want to be casual," I blurt.

She stops breathing.

"I want us to be real, with feelings and permanence. I want us to—"

"Me, too," she blurts.

It's my turn to stare owlishly at her.

"You do? I thought…"

Sadie lifts a shoulder, trying to play it off as ambivalence, but I can see the anxiety in her eyes. "Lu talked some sense into me."

"Remind me to thank her," I tease, before I rake my hand through her waves to cup the back of her head. "What else did she say?"

She fists her hands in my hoodie. "Something along the lines of I was being a dumb-dumb."

"Really? A dumb-dumb?"

She nods. "Really."

"Fuck, I love you," I blurt.

Sadie's eyes go wide. Her entire body goes tense.

Shit. I just ruined this.

But then she gives a sigh and her whole body melts into mine.

"I love you, too," she says.

It's my turn to blink a few times. "Wh-what?" I can't possibly have heard that correctly.

Why isn't she running for the hills?

"I love you," Sadie says, and it's the sweetest sound I've ever heard.

———

We barely make it inside her apartment before clothes are flying. I've never felt need like this, all-consuming. She tries to pull me onto the couch when I force myself to take a step back and breathe.

"What's wrong?" Sadie's panting, her shirt gone and leaving her in a plain beige bra.

It's the hottest thing I've ever seen.

Swallowing hard, I take her by the hand and half-pull, half-drag her into the bedroom. She lets out a little squeal when I pick her up and toss her onto the bed.

Settling on my knees on the floor, I pull off her sneakers and socks, running my finger up the arch of her foot. She lets out a soft sigh and I can see the way she collapses, boneless, onto the bed.

Working first one foot and then the other, I massage away her tension before I slide my hands up her calves and thighs.

She lifts her head up when I reach her waist, and as I pull the tight spandex of her leggings down her hips, she lifts to help. I press a kiss to her belly, just beneath her belly button, and then trail my mouth lower, over the crease of her hip and thigh, and down lower, making my way to the sensitive skin on her inner thighs.

"Jared…" She sighs, her hands tunneling into my hair.

"Yes, my love?"

Her eyes flutter open. I pause, my mouth hovering over her center.

Sadie beams. "Say it again."

"My love?"

Her pleased smile stretches from ear to ear as she sinks back onto the pillows. "I love you," she says, like she can't believe it's actually true.

"I love you, too," I tell her, before I pull her panties down and fuse my mouth to her center.

She jerks at the unexpected pressure. There's a time for sweet and slow. That's not now.

Playtime is never over until she's had her fill—multiple times. And I don't know how long I can drag it out tonight.

Sliding two fingers into her tight, wet heat, she lets out a moan and rides my hand. Her rich scent envelops me, driving me crazy. I have to reach down and press the heel of my hand against my cock before I come in my pants like an overeager teenager.

This isn't about me; it's about her. I won't be satisfied until she is.

As I twist my fingers and find that spongy spot that drives her wild, Sadie moans, long and loud. Her walls flutter around me and she throws her head back, her fingers tightening in my hair almost painfully.

Breathing hard, she lays back on the bed, her arms splayed above her head. I wait for her to give me the go-ahead nod before I withdraw my fingers from within her, licking them clean. I can never get enough of her taste.

I curl up beside her on the bed, pulling her into my arms. Just holding her feels fantastic after a week away. I could lay like this with her forever.

After she's had a few moments to catch her breath and

indulge in some snuggles, Sadie sets a hand on my bare chest and gives me a light shove.

"Yes?"

"Pants off," she says.

"You don't want another?"

She shakes her head. "I just want you."

As I roll off the bed to shuck my pants, she grabs a condom from the bedside table and tosses it my way.

I have no issues with continuing to use condoms. It's safer, yes, but also, it's less messy to clean up for myself. If she decides she wants to carry my brother's baby as their surrogate, we'll discuss alternatives, but I want things to be as painless as possible for her.

Would I like to see my cum dripping down her thigh? Yes. Does it bother me that I don't get to? No, not really. There are so many other things we can do and play, the so-called "loss" of that act isn't enough for me to walk away.

Using condoms doesn't mean we're not committed or in love. It just means we're taking extra precautions. Neither of us wants to raise a child. I'm not quite ready for a vasectomy yet—but when the time comes, I'll be there bright and early to get it taken care of.

And as I crawl back onto the bed and roll on the latex, Sadie immediately rolls over to me, pulling me down on top of her. I'm careful to keep my weight off of her.

"I want you," she says, need tinging her voice. "I want all of you."

Pulling back just enough to maneuver, I notch the tip of my cock at her entrance.

The slow, smooth glide of my cock inside of her feels like heaven. Her eyes roll back in her head, her back arched as she takes me.

thirty

. . .

Sadie

HOLY FUCK.

I thought sex with Jared was pretty good before. We get along great, the chemistry is fire, and he knows exactly what I need to come over and over again.

But sex with the man I'm in love with? Sex with the man who loves me back?

There's nothing like it. I've never experienced this before.

My hand reaches for him, and as he links our fingers together, I squeeze his hand so tight I can barely breathe.

We're connected in every way possible. His cock inside of me, his big body surrounding me, his breath puffing against my lips, his hand in mine, his scent enveloping me. It's a heady type of high.

I never want this to end.

And as he pulls back and thrusts slowly back inside, I realize that it doesn't have to. We can keep doing this forever.

We agreed to casual. We agreed to two days at a time.

Now, I think I'm ready to think more long-term.

I don't know what that looks like for us. I still don't want to get married, and I know I don't want kids. Can we just do this forever?

Jared kisses me, drawing me back into the moment. Wrapping my legs around his waist, I meet him thrust for thrust, the slick slip and slide of our bodies sending me soaring.

We have plenty of sex. It gives him pleasure to bring me pleasure, and we're not shy about trying new things. We have a whole chest of toys we've played with.

But this? This isn't sex.

This is making love.

The intimacy should scare me. Not long ago, it would have made me run away.

Fuck, I almost did.

Now… I love him. And he loves me. And he's not leaving.

There's no reason to be scared. My heart feels full, so full it might burst like a balloon pumped with too much helium.

I'm not high on helium. I'm high on *love*.

"Fuck, Sadie," he says. His free hand digs into my hip. "You're killing me here."

I drag my focus back to where we're connected. "I don't want to kill you," I tease. "I just want to love you."

Something like awe crosses over his face. "I want to love you, too."

"Move in with me." The words come out before I realize I'm saying them. Now that they're out there… they feel right.

Jared lets out a choked laugh. "Now?" He rolls his hips, his cock deep inside me.

"Yes. Now. Right this minute," I declare with a laugh.

He groans. "We're going to have to table this discussion."

"Is—is that a no?"

"It's a 'I can't think straight when I'm inside of you,'" he says.

He pulls out, maneuvering me onto my hands and knees. Sliding his cock home again, he wraps his arms around my middle, holding me tight.

"It's a yes, by the way," he says, his voice hoarse in my ear.

"Yeah?" I twist to see his face.

"Always a yes with you," Jared says. He kisses me softly. "Now, I'm going to fuck you. Is that okay?" He has a teasing smirk on his lips.

"Yes, please."

And then he fucks me.

Later, when we're sated and sweaty, Jared runs his hand up and down my spine.

"Were you serious?"

"About what?" I prop my head on his pec to look up at him.

"Moving in."

"Yes. I want you here. I want you in my bed," I tell him definitively.

I didn't know how much I needed it until now.

"My job… I'm only on a temp contract. I don't…"

"I'm not worried about that."

Jared arches an eyebrow. "You're not?"

"You'll find a job. And I can work from anywhere. If we have to, we can relocate."

It would suck to leave his brother and all our friends, but we could do it.

Together.

"The bookstore…"

"It's a job," I tell him. "I want to be with *you*, not the store. I'm sure there are bookstores in whatever city we end up in."

"I want to stay here," he says firmly.

"Then we'll stay here," I agree. "Whatever we need to make it work, we'll do it."

He kisses me, soft and sweet. "I fucking love you."

"I fucking love you, too."

epilogue

· · ·

Jared

three years later

THE HOSPITAL ROOM smells like antiseptic, the sharp, stinging scent punching me in the face.

Sadie is in the hospital bed, a bundle of blankets in her arms. I move to stand beside her, my hand on her shoulder. Trailing a finger over the baby's downy soft cheek, I marvel at the fact that she made this, she did this.

"We could keep her," I tell her, my voice hoarse.

"We're not keeping her," Sadie laughs.

"We could, though… Nobody would have to know."

At the other side of the bed, my brother squeaks. "I would know!"

"Come here, Yo-Yo," Sadie tells him. She's adopted my nickname for him. "Come meet your baby."

Elliott stands beside Yoni, visibly choked up. They set their hand on his arm.

"That's our kid," they say. "We did it." They look up at Sadie. "*We* did. All of us."

When Yoni and Elliott decided they would take Sadie up on her offer of egg donation and surrogacy, they were all a little worried about how I'd take it. Not many guys would be okay with their partner having a baby with someone else. Especially when it's his brother.

But she isn't having a baby *with* Yoni. She donated her eggs and her body. I couldn't be more proud of her for doing so.

And knowing she did this to help my brother? To give him the dream he's always wanted?

The second she agreed to doing this thing long-term with me, I scheduled a vasectomy. It helped to make sure we wouldn't have any oopsies while she was on the intense fertility drugs before the egg retrieval and then the implantation. I was on the fence about kids before, but knowing she doesn't want them for herself, it was an easy call. I'd rather have her than not, and if that means no kids, I'm perfectly happy to live our life that way.

Yoni and Elliott have five more embryos. I don't think they want five more kids, some might not work out, but if they do... I'm on board. As many as she wants, I'll stand beside her and hold her hand every step of the way.

Watching her give my brother a baby? I've never been more in awe of her strength and resilience.

And let me just say—sex with a perpetually horny woman high on hormones? I could barely keep up with her. Every night was a marathon.

Sadie sets the baby in Yoni's arms. His eyes go wide and glassy with unshed tears.

"Hi, baby," he whispers. He runs his pinkie finger along her hand, and I watch as the baby clutches at him.

A lump forms in my throat and I squeeze Sadie's shoulder again. Her eyes are leaking tears.

Oh, to hell with all of it. I let the tears fall.

The four of us stand there, blubbering silently, as the most perfect little angel sits in my brother's arms, taking the world in.

"Have you thought about a name?" Sadie asks.

"Aviva," Elliott says firmly.

My heart catches in my throat. "After Nonna?" That was our grandmother's name.

Yoni nods. He was always close with her, even more so than I was, and I was a straight up grandma's boy.

He passes my niece to Elliott, and I watch as my brother and his spouse become parents right in front of my eyes. It's magical.

I never thought I'd be lucky to have this. Our little family is unconventional, that's for sure. Our family of origin wasn't enough for us; we went out and built our own family.

Yoni and Elliott. Asher and Arielle. Rachel, Sullivan, and all the book club friends.

We've found each other. We've found our home.

Sadie reaches for me and I sit on the edge of her hospital bed. I run a hand through her tangled hair and press a kiss to her temple.

"I love you," I murmur, and she smiles, a tired joy spreading across her face.

"I love you, more," she counters.

"Impossible."

———

In this bonus epilogue, Jared goes to a book signing with Sadie and generally makes a nuisance of himself. Luckily, she likes it. Mostly.

afterword

Thank you for reading *Sportsball is for Lovers*. This book is my baby and I absolutely love it to pieces.

Reviews are more important than readers realize. If you liked this book, please leave me a review!

<u>Join my newsletter</u> to stay in the loop! Lots of unfunny quips, unsuccessful attempts at wit, and general grouching about the writing process.

xoxo,

Allie

what's next?

Thank you for reading *Sportsball is for Lovers*.

Want more enemies to lovers? Check out *Ruck Me Harder*. Tony is a grumpy gymnast. Viv is the even grumpier rugby superstar he hooked up with at the Olympics three years ago… and never called back.

For more neurodivergent love stories, check out *The Thought of You*, where Johanna discovers she's autistic when her reformed playboy roommate tells her.

In your hockey era? Check out *Puck Me Twice*, featuring Vanessa and the autistic hockey player she asks to be her fake boyfriend, not knowing he wants it to be real.

about the author

Allie is a queer and AuDHD writer with a hyper-fixation on inclusivity and representation. She loves the color purple, Michigan football, the Detroit Lions, and the Boston Bruins. When she's not absorbed by a book, she likes to spend time with her nephews.

A San Diego, CA native now residing in South Carolina, she is allergic to the cold, rain, snow, and mosquitos.